Gregg —

Xmas ,

RAT

RAT

A Novel
by

Andrzej Zaniewski

Translated from the Polish by
EWA HRYNIEWICZ-YARBROUGH

ARCADE PUBLISHING • *New York*

FIRST ENGLISH-LANGUAGE EDITION

Library of Congress Cataloging-in-Publication Data
Zaniewski, Andrzej.
    Rat : a novel / by Andrzej Zaniewski ; translated from the
Polish by Ewa Hryniewicz-Yarbrough. — 1st English-language
ed.
        p.   cm.
    ISBN 1-55970-262-1
    1. Rats — Fiction.   I. Hryniewicz-Yarbrough, Ewa.   II.
Title.
PG7185.A5R38   1994
891.8′537 — dc20   94-9937

Published in the United States by Arcade Publishing, Inc.,
New York
Distributed by Little, Brown and Company

10 9 8 7 6 5 4 3 2 1

BP

Designed by API

PRINTED IN THE UNITED STATES OF AMERICA

I think we are in rats' alley
Where the dead men lost their bones.

T. S. Eliot, *The Wasteland*

Foreword

D ear reader: *Rat* is my first novel about animals, a novel devoted to exceptional and little-known creatures, since human knowledge of rodents has more to do with the methods of exterminating them than with understanding their behavior, their psyche and emotions. At the same time it is a novel full of sensation and mystery, because many tragedies, dramas, adventures, take place around rats' burrows and nests: the exploits of Hercules, the tragedy of Oedipus, the wanderings of Odysseus, the despair of Niobe, the death of Antigone, the fates of gods, Titans, and humans, clash, interweave, connect, making us aware of what is great and important to our hearts.

We don't want to remember it in our seemingly pure human world. Rats arouse revulsion and dread, fear of the diseases they sometimes transmit, and an almost superstitious terror at the power of their constantly growing teeth. The existence of the underground community of rats, their adaptability and constant struggle for survival, their mass wanderings and individual propensity for traveling, the instances of their unusual intelligence, the legends and stories I have listened to since childhood — all that has contributed to my fascination with rats and aroused not only my curiosity but also a certain admiration and respect for nature, which created these animals that coexist so well with people.

Rattus norvegicus and *Rattus rattus,* the "domestic" rat and the gray rat — the two basic species of the great rat family — have accompanied humankind since the beginning of its existence. Their fate is closely linked with our fate, and to a large extent it reflects our own level of civilization and our ecological situation. It seems strange that these rodents have found the most congenial living conditions near people, who from the beginning have declared war on them. Inhabiting caves, forests, and steppes, the weak creatures were easy prey for birds, snakes, and predatory mammals, but on contact with people they transformed themselves, they grew in strength, started their collective attack.

Contrary to widespread opinion, people create favorable conditions for rats, and only thanks to our civilization have rats conquered all the continents and reached such an advanced level of social organization. Our cellars, warehouses, granaries, garbage containers, dumps, stables, military barracks, prisons, farms, sewers, dams, kitchens, and garages have become home to rats, their kingdom, and maybe the place of birth of an upcoming civilization that will be unusually strong and fecund, predacious and resistant to any changes that take place in the surrounding world.

I have always been intrigued by the causes and mechanisms that determine rats' existence, their social structures and the dependencies among individuals, their diverse personalities and dispositions, which are almost identical with those of humans. In laboratory experiments, each rat placed in a maze behaves differently: he reveals his talents and weaknesses; sometimes he gives up, escapes, or withdraws, and sometimes, maybe more often, he searches for an exit, makes a conscious choice to gnaw through the thin walls in order to create or discover a new maze.

I have tried to get close to rats, to get to know them as well as possible. I raised them, I watched them, I tried to understand them and make friends with them. I have seen rats inhabiting the ruins of postwar Gdansk and the moldering houses of the city's New Port, rats trying to get onto ships, descending and climbing mooring cables. I have watched rats in the alleys of Saigon, Istanbul, Berlin, Bucharest, Warsaw, and many other cities. I have also collected all possible information and gossip about their life and habits. I have assumed that if I accept even the untrue elements of particular legends and tales, I will get to know not only rats but also people, who have created those stories out of disgust or hatred, or, conversely, out of admiration, friendship, or faith.

Buddhism, for example, places the rat relatively high in the hierarchy of living creatures. Jumping off the ox's back, the sly and cunning rat is the first to appear before the dying Buddha. Following the rat — the most intelligent animal — and the ox — the hardest-working — the other animals of the Buddhist calendar appear: the tiger, the rabbit, the dragon, the snake, the horse, the rooster, the sheep, the monkey, the dog, and the wild boar.

Another legend tells about thousands of rats from the Karai Ma temple in Bikaner, in the west of India. Those rats are the dead poets who, in their animal incarnation, wait to assume their shape of poet-bards.

The character of a villainous ruler eaten by the army of mice or rats shows up in the legends of many nations. We can surmise that those legends are based on real events. We can also assume that the multitudes of those rodents that were described by the German traveler Peter Pallas, who saw them swimming across the Volga in the vicinity of Astrakhan in the spring of 1721, had already surmounted land and water obstacles as they wandered in search of new territories and food across Asia, Europe, and Africa.

It was not only our legendary Polish prince Popiel who was devoured by mice. Hatte I, the archbishop of Mainz, burned a group of starving, destitute people to save food for his court. For that evil deed he was eaten by mice in the tower on the Rhine that to this day has been known as Binger Maüseturm. A similar, well-deserved fate befell many other rulers, as well as both ecclesiastical and lay notables, their stories gleefully told in the legends of different nations. Yet starving rats that devour people belong not only to the realm of legends but also to the realm of facts. Adventurers and treasure seekers who explore old dungeons, forts, and cellars, as well as workers in sewers and tunnels, are well aware of that. In 1977, when I was staying in war-ravaged, starving Vietnam, I heard of rats consuming children left by overworked mothers in seemingly safe cradles.

The rat's fate, always alongside human fate, is a recurring motif in many books — in Kafka, Eliot, Joyce, Camus. The careful reader will find echoes of those episodes, anecdotes, and legends, and their further elaboration, in *Rat* — a cruel new Odyssey, written many years ago.

The main idea behind my private philosophy is the conviction that all forms of life on earth originate from the same source and are the descendants of the same mystery of existence, the mystery of purpose and significance. I believe that animals as intelligent as rats are guided not only by their instinct and reflexes but also by their own intellect, experience, associations, memory, and emotions; that they can draw conclusions from facts and surrounding phenomena; that they are less animalistic and more human than we humans, in our arrogance, are willing to admit. The self-styled or divinely appointed lords of creation, human beings should be tolerant protectors and friends of the billions of creatures whose languages they don't understand and whose behavior they judge according to schemes that are convenient for them. Unfortunately, the reverse is true. And yet we know that the existence and life of each of us depends on the same protein compounds as the dog's life, the rat's, the pigeon's, and every other living creature's. People forget that they are the same organisms as animals, and act as if they wanted to reject this inconvenient kinship and to deny their biological roots at any cost. As a result, they search for the origins of their existence beyond the boundaries of our galaxy or in the breath of the Supreme Being. That only attests to their extreme arrogance and to the unjustified feeling of superiority that is grounded only in the imagination.

We believe that our civilization is supreme and perfect, the first and the last. This blind faith is the error that we commit daily. We don't know what civilization the future will bring, when, consciously or unconsciously, we will commit collective suicide, a not-so-distant possibility. Maybe it will be a civilization of rats, maybe of birds, or maybe of insects.

We have long stopped seeing partners in animals. We view them only as biological elements that should be subordinated to our will, our knowledge, and our whims. We judge the animal's intelligence insofar as it submits to us. We have built huge slaughterhouses, farms, tanning factories, millions of places of destruction. We are not only arrogant but also the most cruel of all nature's creatures, and we consider that as normal or even as good form, as we do the wearing of elegant fox furs or coats made of aborted astrakhan lambs. I'm writing about those issues because it might be worth our while to realize who we really are and where we are really going.

If you, dear reader, believe at times in reincarnation, you may also believe that a person who was a rat in his earlier incarnation carries the memory of that existence in his subconscious, that the outline of his previous life superimposes itself in unusual and dramatic situations on his present life, human and therefore distant from the former. If, however, you reverse this situation and imagine a spirit that left its human body and found its subsequent earthly existence in the body of a rat, you may go one step further and discover that your own consciousness has undergone such a transformation. If you do that, you yourself will become the hero of my novel and you will understand how much you have in common with that seemingly alien and distant animal. Then everything that I have written will become simple and obvious.

This book is both a description based on facts and a fairy tale, a legend, exceptionally cruel and strange, gray and painful like a rat's life and therefore plausible. Living next to us, literally under our feet, the community of rodents has accompanied us for thousands of years. It has participated in our welfare and in our poverty, in peace and in war. We don't want to see them, we don't want to know about them. We fight them, we despise them as only we humans are capable of despising.

I wonder whether the camouflage of some of my hero's actions, of many events and motifs, isn't too impenetrable, whether, woven into the contemporary landscape, the symbols of the past, the traces going back to the beginnings of civilization, will be interpreted correctly.

Rat is not exclusively a book about animals, even though such an interpretation may also be acceptable. On the contrary, it is a novel about the laws that govern society, about our mythologies, our truths and lies, about love and hope, loneliness and nostalgia. We inhabit after all the same cosmos, breathe the same earthly atmosphere, belong to the same class of mammals, with a similarly structured brain, heart, and stomach, a similar process of impregnation and maternity. We are then relatives, very close biologically and psychologically. And even though different causes have been responsible, both our species, thanks to their vitality, strength, and intelligence, have not only survived millions of years of evolution but also taken control of our planet.

Don't forget, then, dear reader, that in describing a rat's life in this detailed, naturalistic way, I had you in mind.

RAT

Darkness, like the darkness after birth, darkness all around. Back then it was even darker: a black, impenetrable barrier separated me from life, from open space, from consciousness. I knew nothing except darkness, unlike now, when afterimages, traces of light, remnants, fragments, shadows, glow in the brain.

Try to recall that first darkness that you have seen and remembered, summon it up in its first, earliest shape, try to re-create the course of life, the events, the wanderings, the escapes, the travels — from the first moments after leaving Mother's warm belly, from the first painful, choking breath of air, from the experience of sudden cold, from the cutting of the umbilical cord and the gentle touch of the tongue.

I remember: sewers, cellars, basements, caverns, attics, tunnels, passageways, cracks, gutters, sewage pits, septic tanks, ditches, drains, wells, garbage containers, refuse dumps, warehouses, pantries, henhouses, pigpens, cow-sheds, barns. . . . My rat's world — a life submerged in shade, blackness, grayness, dusk and darkness, twilight and night, farthest from the day, from light, from the blinding sun, from brightness, from piercing rays, from shiny and dazzling surfaces.

Farthest from light — when only the smell of milk in the swollen teats and the warmth of the belly led me, when the sealed conchae of my ears let in no sounds — then for the first time, through the thin membrane of eyelids that were grown together, I saw a gray shadow, a lighter patch in the deep surrounding darkness. It was the gleam of a light bulb or refracted sunlight falling in at noon through the cellar window, which suddenly reached my closed eyes, stirring the first premonitions.

The soft light fascinates, captivates, beckons. You tear yourself away from the mammary gland and crawl clumsily toward the glow.

With her teeth, Mother gently grasps me by the skin, draws me near, lays me down next to her. Close to the warm milky belly, you forget the gray patch. You forget it only for a moment. Soon the anxiety returns, again I see the dim contour, once more I tear myself away and crawl toward the tunnel connecting the nest with the cellar.

Mother licks me all over, washes me with her moist tongue, removes the first fleas that have already nestled in my groin.

I remember little about those distant beginnings of consciousness, when I was yet unaware that I was a rat and the dormant imagination could not intuit or explain anything.

Besides pursuing light, pursuing all the bright light that penetrates my eyelids, I respond to Mother's shrill squeaks. Those squeaks, as much as the smell of the mammary glands and the sense of safe warmth, lure, instruct, and command me.

My hearing hasn't developed yet; the ear openings are grown together, and only a fraction of the sounds reaches inside. Still, you immediately recognize Mother's squeaking, you associate it with warmth and the delicious taste of milk.

Up till now my pink skin has been hairless, but it slowly sprouts delicate gray down. I feel warmer and warmer. I am no longer afraid to lie uncovered.

2

I grow, get stronger. I reach the milk-filled teat first and push aside those crawling nearby. I shove them back, block their way, and when the gland is empty, with my whole weight I crawl to the next one.

I eat the most, I am the biggest. Other young rats yield, surrender. Each day I strive to stand, to straighten the still-unwieldy paws, to move forward and back, to turn over and get up. When I succeed, I squeak to call Mother, who pulls me to herself, grabbing my tail or the skin on my back with her teeth.

The need for a hard surface on which I can learn to walk becomes as urgent as the need for light in my eyes, closed but more and more sensitive.

Here on the hard bottom of the nest I sense the claws growing out of my paws, still weak, bending easily, resilient, helping me to get up.

Mother washes my body with her tongue, removes all impurities and feces, catches the fleas whose bites pain me. The next time she grooms me, the conchae of my ears open. Suddenly all the surrounding sounds reach me. The humming of the faucet, the creaking of the stairs, the blows on the sewage pipes, the cries of young rats, the distant noise of the street, the nocturnal meowing of a cat, the high tide of murmurs, echoes, voices, rustlings, tremors, movements.

Stunned, I sprawl at the bottom of the nest, lift my head, and call for help. For the first time I clearly hear my own voice — a piercing, vibrating cry. Until now I have perceived it differently — muffled, distant alongside Mother's voice, the loudest voice of all. Now, among the many sounds coming from all directions, it seems feeble and faint. The light that penetrates my eyelids continues to remain a mystery, unexplained and unintelligible. Now all the young rats seek the gray, reddish patches, and Mother has an unusually hard time with us: she is always vigilant and prevents us from crawling out of the burrow. Since our legs keep getting stronger and stronger, this is particularly troublesome. Although sluggish and slow, we can already move all over the nest. Exasperated, Mother lies down at the exit, trying to block the way. We clamber over her back and crawl in the direction of the unknown, enticing grayness, which spins faster and faster under our eyelids. Several young rats have disappeared, and each of us has his own mammary gland, whereas earlier, near Mother's belly, we kept pushing, prodding, and shoving each other away.

Maybe Mother herself has devoured a few young ones that have become permeated by an alien smell and lost the scent of the nest. Maybe, continually pushed away from the teat, they have died of hunger and exhaustion. Maybe they have crawled down the tunnel toward the light, and a cat has snatched them. Maybe another female rat, whose own litter has perished, has stolen them. . . .

Several spirited males and females have remained, increasingly impatient with their blindness, helplessness, weakness, and inadaptability.

We can already recognize our own smell and the touch of the whiskers — stiff and sensitive bristles that grow from the nostrils.

The muscles of the eyelids, immobile so far, begin to contract, move, strain. I try to open, unclench, raise them.

Mother helps us, wiping and cleaning the eye area with her tongue. To the light, with all strength to the light.

I can see. My eyelids are opening. First, through a small crack, a diffused ray of light seeps inside. I experience a strange sensation: the light reveals the sculpted surface of the ground, the interior of the nest, the burrow, the tunnels leading in different directions. I can see clearly what up to now I could smell, sense with my whiskers, feel with my skin, and touch with my paws. The details, the creases, furrows, ovals, ridges, folds, elevations, swellings, acquire a different meaning. The visible shape differs in the inexhaustible wealth of its brightness from the shape that is touched. Light cannot be imagined if it has never been seen.

I can see. My lids open further, they slide off the bulbous eyeballs. The greatest discovery — the discovery of my own self. I carefully examine my own anatomy: the claws growing from my hairless toes, the back, which I can see when I turn my head, the tail, consisting of delicate rings, the budding genitals, the dark fluffy fur that's lighter on the belly. I look at Mother's sweet-smelling teats, her soft, warm belly under which I can hide, her powerful teeth that gently grasp my skin.

You are a young rat that lives in an underground nest, a rat whose mother watches you and protects you from dangers that you don't know and can't foresee.

I don't know yet what fear means; I only know the short-lived fear caused by hunger when Mother takes too long to return to the nest.

That happened several times when you lay far away and couldn't reach the milk-filled glands. You were afraid then that you wouldn't find them. When, after returning, Mother drew you to herself, you fed and felt the joy of being satisfied. That sensation had to do with satiety. Full and lazy, feeling the delightful warmth of milk in my belly, by myself I moved away from the warm teats.

I can see. I'm surrounded by black, concave, uneven surfaces, with openings to the dark tunnels that lead in different directions. You can move in them only with the help of the whiskers. The tunnels end abruptly at blind walls. Only the tunnel through which a shiny glow enters leads farther. I don't yet know where, and that uncertainty troubles and puzzles me most. For the present, Mother and Father forbid me to approach this mysterious opening, and when I try to run fast outside, they punish me by biting my ears. Out of necessity, I romp inside, visit blind corridors, play with other young rats, exercise my teeth on a rotten board.

The light keeps luring me. I want to know its source, its nature, to find out exactly what it is.

Slowly I begin to understand that its changing intensity, its brightness and hue, depend on the events taking place behind the windows. Sometimes it is dazzling and sharp, with its bright reflection lighting up the interior as far as the walls that narrow at the top. At other times it is misty, unvarying, slanting in at a different angle. I have also watched violent changes in the beams of light, as if their source were pulsating. What amazed me most, though, was the regular absence of light. But for the time being, Mother thwarted all my attempts at going out and examining those mysterious phenomena.

When was it that I began to fear light? The fear came later. At first I became suspicious and distrustful. A young rat sneaks out, goes outside.

Mother, who always leaps out after each of us, this time remains on the spot, raises her nostrils, moves her whiskers. She is upset. With her whole body she blocks the tunnel. Her anxiety passes on to us. We huddle by her side.

A distant squeaking, scuffling, meowing. I can smell the alien, unpleasant odor that disturbs Mother so much. The squeaking stops. I wait for it to come back. It doesn't. Mother cuddles us under her belly, covers us, crawls over us, stretches her neck, sniffs. A cat has entered the cellar through the broken window. He keeps watch, lurking behind the faucet. He prowls, he knows we are there. But we, young restless rats, know nothing about him, we are not aware of the impending danger, we don't associate the disappearance of a little rat with the cat's smell. We are only disturbed by Mother's behavior, by her nervousness, by the acrid taste of the formerly sweet milk. The light lures. So again we try to get out, unsuspecting of danger, unaware of the existence of enemies, poisons, traps, with no inkling of death, unaware that death is possible.

I grow stronger, bigger, more active. There, behind the thin wall of the cellar, another world, a new, unknown reality, exists. From there the parents bring food, from there comes Father, whom Mother now permits to spend the night in the nest. I have to go out, I must go out no matter what. The cat often sneaks in, lurks in the cellar. Mother then shivers with fear, and we crawl under her belly. Soon another heedless young rat is eaten by the cat.

People have replaced the broken windowpane, and the cat can't get in any longer.

Mother leads me out straight into the light. The beam descending from the high opening strikes my pupils and blinds me. I rest at the entrance in a bright circle. I discover that besides radiance, light carries warmth. For a long while I savor that streak of light. But the bright spot disappears suddenly, reappears after a moment, disappears one more time, shifts again. We are now running over the cellar. Clumsily we climb the piled-up blocks of coal, we slide down, fall, spring at each other in sham attacks. Water gurgles in the faucet. Mother walks up to a big slab, slides under it. I follow her cautiously. Water glistens in the dark. Mother bends down, drinks. A young careless rat jumps straight into the water. He squeals, terrified. He moves his legs, tries to swim. Mother grabs him by the back with her teeth and pulls him up. The cellar is spacious, I run around it many times. You can squeeze under the door to the other side. Now that I know which way the light reaches the cellar, I must find out what is behind the door, in the darkness from which people come. Steps on the stairs. Mother grabs me and carries me toward the burrow. The other rats run after us. Now we listen to the sounds from the cellar.

I already know the noise made by the key. But the creaking of the hinges in the window is a new sound. Cool, moist air reaches the nest. I move my nostrils. Many unfamiliar sounds squeeze into my ears. The rumbling sound made by the coal being unloaded into the cellar muffles all other sounds and echoes. It bores through the ears, splits the skull. Choking dust fills the nest. Terrified, together with other rats, I scurry all over the nest. Finally I cling to the cold wall at the end of the blind tunnel. Mother is unperturbed — she must have earlier become used to the rumble. She watches us so that in panic we won't dash outside.

The shovels rattle. The blocks of coal fall down. The dust settles. The people leave the cellar. Friction when the key turns. Silence, sudden silence. Mother cautiously sticks her head outside, moves her whiskers, draws air into her nostrils. She checks to see if the danger is still there, if the people have left. We crouch behind her long, hairless tail. At last she leads us outside. I notice that the light coming into the cellar through the dusty window has moved near the door.

*   *   *

I can already differentiate between day and night. I can differentiate between the light connected with human presence and light that comes through the window. I know that beyond the walls of the nest, beyond the walls of the house in which I was born, an unknown world exists. I know it by the shadows blurring the brightness of the light, by the scent of Mother and Father returning from the outside, by the smell entering through the open doors and windows, by the sounds in the sewage pipes, by the murmurs, echoes, squeaks, creaks, by the rattling and grinding.

Unfamiliar rats come to the cellar. Their smell, though similar to ours in some ways, is different. Chasing them away, Mother bites at them. The strange rats bring the scent of their own nests, the smell of their own different routes, of their families. I try to skulk after them, to follow their tracks. I am enraged when Mother pulls me away from the door of the cellar and carries me to the nest.

Day after day, night after night. Curiosity turns into compulsion. The urge to leave the cellar and go farther pushes me in the direction of the oblong crack under the door. All the young rats are excited and restless. Feigned assaults, escapes, fights, happen more and more often. With our legs we push each other away, we claw each other, roll over, bite ears, noses, tails, bellies.

We get to know the intoxicating taste of blood, the unique taste, the taste of mouse meat and the taste of the bird that was still alive when Father brought it.

The smallest and the weakest of the young rats sneaks out through the crack under the cellar door. He returns smeared with pungent liquid. The odor overpowers his natural rat's smell, by which we recognize each other. He is alien, different. We now acquire experience by attacking the smallest and the weakest among us. The sharp teeth strike his eye. Blinded, he hides in the corner. Soon his skin is covered with a layer of coagulated blood and scabbing wounds. We bite him, chase him, claw him as if he didn't come from our family. Mother won't stand up in his defense, won't even let him hide under her belly.

After another chase, the blood-covered rat dies squeezed between blocks of coal.

The cellar gets smaller and smaller. I make up my mind to break out of it as soon as possible.

I set out along the cellar wall covered with grooved, chipped plaster. I am summoned by distant smells, light whiffs of the unknown world, trails of different air. At first I move cautiously, as if I were surrounded by menacing dangers, as if in each grayness, each spiderweb, each furrow, each bend of the wall, an unknown enemy were lurking. I fear everything I don't know. A spider runs across my path. I touch it with the tips of the whiskers — it cringes, grows still, turns into a lump of earth.

Its fear helps me. It is more scared than I, it is weaker than I, more delicate, fragile. . . . A movement of the incisors will be enough to take its life. No, there's no need for that. I did see Mother walk around such motionless gray clods. They must be untasty or unwholesome.

I leave the motionless spider and more boldly continue on my way. I slip between the wall and the sewage pipe, which is wrapped in oakum. Suddenly I hear a murmur, which grows louder and louder, as if something were rushing toward me. Sharp, violent sounds reverberate in the pipe, and a powerful, hissing, gurgling stream rolls over my head.

Frantic, I cling to the wall as if I were really in peril. The sounds pierce, recede, vanish. For a moment I desperately want to flee.

The feeling of fear is gone almost immediately. I keep

walking. I feel the cold breeze much more strongly now. It comes from the bright border that surrounds the door visible on the horizon. I stop every now and then, look around, go on. My nostrils register the waft of colder air carrying entirely new, delicious, appetizing smells. Abruptly I feel sharp teeth on my back. Mother holds me tight by the skin, picks me up, turns me over. I squeal from anger. My paws hang in the air, my tail sweeps the floor. Mother has decided that it is still too early for me to go out by myself.

I turn my head and try to grab her ear with my teeth.

We are going back. Mother stops as if she has sensed danger among the blows, reverberations, and echoes that come from above.

Distant rhythmic sounds. They grow more resonant as they approach. Mother retreats between the wall and the cluster of thin pipes.

The opened door creaks. Sharp light fills the space, reaching the ceiling, which is covered with cobwebs and soot. A gust of warm air terrifies Mother so much that she almost squeezes into the wall. She places me before herself on the concrete. The pressure exerted by her teeth never slackens.

The people bring in a large wooden crate. Their puffing and mumbling frighten me. I squeal with fear. Mother lets go of my skin and crawls on top of me. She covers me, drowns all the sounds. She sweats, her smell changes, alarms me. The sound of her blood is also different — faster, nervous. Her veins become engorged.

Those gurgling and puffing lumps of meat must be dangerous to us.

They place the crate in front of the door to the cellar, where the entrance to our burrow is. They open the door wide, push an iron weight against it to keep it from closing. I thrust my head from under Mother's belly. I want to see.

11

Vexed, she pushes my head under again. The route to the burrow is closed.

Right now more thumping can be heard from the stairs. Another group is toting a crate. Yelling, crashing, puffing.

People, it's people — our greatest enemies. They stand the crate next to us.

I see people for the first time, I smell them for the first time, I am close to them for the first time. I hear the heavy thumping of human hearts. The sour scent of sweat fills the cellar.

Noisy, shapeless, with legs that bend, with stiffly mounted round heads, they emit mumbling, hissing sounds. Mother is nervous. Again she grabs my back with her teeth. She turns around and runs toward the sewage pipes.

We have succeeded. Squeezed between pipes bandaged with oakum and plastered, we feel a little safer. Mother's blood pumps more slowly. It almost returns to its normal rhythm. But the people are still menacing. Their presence, their smell, the light they have brought, agitate us. We are surrounded. Open overhead, the space between the pipes and the wall is not a dependable hiding place.

Mother's nostrils move. Each human has a different, distinct smell. I can smell it when they pass by.

Mother was able to draw many conclusions from that smell — only at the time I didn't know that yet.

We remain motionless, squeezed into a nook between the gurgling pipes and the wall, with no holes to hide in. We wait for the people to leave the cellar, close the door, turn the light off, walk away.

Mother again crawls over me, as if afraid that I will begin to squeak or creep out.

The people are leaving the cellar, they slam the doors, turn the keys in creaking locks. The last person who leaves utters sounds that form a rhythmic sequence of tones.

The light is out. The heavy steps on the stairs recede. The danger is over. Mother calms down. She grasps my neck and carries me straight to the burrow. She lets me go only when we are in the nest, where my scared siblings sniff me with great interest.

The danger has sharpened my hunger. I pounce greedily on the leftovers of the fish that Mother has brought.

It is safe, snug, quiet, warm in the nest — just as in all the nests that you will build in the future.

The first encounter with people has disturbed you, incensed you, scared you. You knew already: a rat's fate is closely, inextricably, permanently bound with human fate — you won't be able to avoid contacts with them.

The puffing, wheezing, mumbling mountains of meat, tottering on their shaking limbs, inspire deadly fear. You need this fear; it will defend you and save you. Learn to fear. Learn to escape. Terror will increase your strength. Later you will learn to hate and kill.

Since that incident, Mother has persistently guarded us. She lies down at the exit, blocking the whole opening with her body, but if, despite that, one of us manages to get out, she grabs his tail and pulls him back in.

Father brings fish heads with wide-open eyes, chicken guts, unfinished slices of bread, scraps of meat.

But the food isn't enough. We grow and we need more and more food, and although everything Father brings is thoroughly ground by our incisors, we begin to experience hunger. At the same time Mother begins to treat us differently. She doesn't let us suck, and each attempt to come near her milk-filled teats ends with a painful bite on the nose or on the tail.

Father brings a live mouse to the nest. I remember his squeaking, much weaker than a rat's. Father must have wanted him to reach the nest alive, because he carried him gently, as if he were his own child. Mauled and scared, the mouse tries to break away, escape, hide in an inaccessible place. He runs, jumps, scrambles over the walls, and finally, realizing that Mother has blocked the only way out, he attempts to surmount the obstacle. Like a ball, he bounces off the opposite wall and leaps on Mother's back. With a swift movement of her teeth, she bites through his throat.

Now she is drinking the blood of the dying mouse, and we draw into our nostrils the unfamiliar smell. We fall upon him, push Mother away, devour what is left.

That first taste of the body that a moment ago was still alive: I remember it well, the warmth and taste of blood that hasn't set yet.

Father brings another live creature — a bird with a broken wing. He lays him down carefully.

Scared by the darkness and the noises, the bird wants to rise; he leaps up, cries.

Starved, we approach, we sniff the chirping bird, we pull him by the feathers, by the beak and the claws, we bite into the thin layer of down.

With the head that you have bitten off, you squat beside the wall. You devour everything, bones and cartilage too. You like best the delicate substance hidden inside the skull, you like the eyes, full of warm, salty liquid.

I was learning to kill, I was learning all my life.

Mother expects a new litter of rats, so she is bent on making us adapt quickly to independent life. She has concluded that if we can kill a wounded bird, we will fare well in the mysterious, unknown outside world.

There is another reason for Mother's changed attitude. She is afraid that we will eat the small, blind, and clumsy newborn rats. You will later find out that many female rats

14

experience that fear. And as earlier she forbade us all contact with the world, now she has started to drive us out from the nest.

This unforeseen change in Mother's moods will determine the fate of our whole group, will determine life and death.

With a little female rat, we set out in search of food. We suffer hunger, and we know that obtaining food means survival. We no longer count on Mother. She shoves us away and even bites us.

Meanwhile our nostrils take in delicious, promising smells from outside. Those magnificent odors make cockroaches and millipedes — the only food available in the cellars — seem bland and monotonous.

We have reached the gurgling pipe where not too long ago I experienced the first encounter with people. Unknown space, full of mysteries, begins beyond.

The keen, sharp, blinding light fascinates us. In our cellar, dim rays seep in through the little dirty window smeared with paint and covered with cobwebs. We have come to the end of that tightly wrapped pipe that disappears into the wall. The terrain here puts us at a disadvantage, because there is nothing to conceal us.

The little female rat moves forward boldly, and I follow with my nose at her tail. Now and then we raise our heads and look around.

The rays coming from the window bend at a sharp angle on the wall. We are cozy, warm, happy.

It is from that small window with the half-broken windowpane that those enticing smells keep coming. We have to get there, we have to climb the old bricks that are piled here. Crates and empty sacks lie on top. A keen, wonderful smell of fresh bread dazes us.

The smell enters together with the light. It seems inseparably linked with it.

The sunken belly of the little female rat moves violently. Thick saliva flows down her gums. I feel increasingly painful hunger. I move my jaws, I clench my teeth, I grind them. The little female has already reached the opening. She disappears over its edge. The small window is high over the ground. I follow her. I'm about to jump. Suddenly, mumbling and hissing sounds stop me. People, it's people. I cling to the window frame.

Bright light falls on the yard paved with gray flagstones. It's harsh, blinding, revealing. Over the roofs I notice a pale, dull space and the ball of the sun, which hurts the eyes.

Dazed by the light, the little female circles the yard, looking for a hiding place, a hole, a nook.

People stand in the open doorway to the bakery. They wave, point, hiss, wheeze, and mumble.

She could easily go under the iron gate that closes off the yard from the street, but she is frightened, disoriented, blinded.

The terrifying noise of cars, steps, conversations, comes from that direction. That's why she retreats. She doesn't even come to the gap between the steel slat in the gate and the concrete. Tin garbage cans stand in the yard.

She tries to hide in one of them. A man in a white apron comes and kicks the tin can. Scared, she runs into the middle of the yard, toward the metal pump that drips water. There is a drain in the depression, but a dense grate bars the opening.

Most likely she has noticed its brown surface from afar. She thinks she will squeeze through it to the other side.

She clings to the metal, bites, claws, presses her nostrils into the hard holes. In vain. The passage is closed, blocked, impossible to cross. Through the grate she sees the dark, moist interior of the drain — the friendly world, familiar and secure.

A man in an untied, rustling, fluttering apron is coming near. Long, fair hair shows from under his cap. He mumbles, snorts, screeches, pants, wheezes.

He is coming. The little female rat lacerates her gums on the metal grate, she tries to bolt, squeeze in, she shakes with fear.

He is coming. In his hand he holds a steaming metal kettle.

He lifts the kettle so high that the shining tin reflects the sun.

The sounds become louder. A stream of scalding water falls on the back of the little female. She tries to escape. It's useless. She rolls over, tumbles down, squirms, writhes. The scalding water flows onto her belly. A squeal pierces the ears. Another stream falls straight on her nostrils. The squealing dies, stops. The man nudges the rat with his foot, he checks, bends over.

He takes the tip of the tail in his two fingers and carries the rat to the garbage can.

He raises the lid, throws the rat in. I turn away, climb down onto the cool concrete floor. I escape. To the nest, to the burrow, to the darkness.

I understand Mother's fear. I know I should fear people all the time, everywhere. At any time, at any place, I should run away from them.

Mother is asleep. I creep in cautiously and begin to gnaw on an uneaten bread crust. This time she puts up with me, she doesn't drive me out. Her massive, balloonlike belly stirs with every breath. The next litter of rats is slowly getting ready to enter the world.

For a long time she has been bringing pieces of cotton wool, shreds of rags, newspapers, string. She pads the new nest for her new offspring.

Father brings a fish that is dry as a bone. When I try to come near the aromatic food, he springs on me and bites me on the neck. I jump aside and run away. There is nothing I can do except leave the nest quickly. I am again on the concrete floor of the cellar. The light seeping in through the lusterless window begins to dim. Night is approaching. I wait amid the heap of broken crates until it gets dark.

Now. Guided by the whiskers protruding from each side of my mouth, I unerringly follow the route I recently covered with the little female.

The yard is lit by a dim lamp. From the cellar window I slowly slip out onto the pavement. Now I know why the little female became disoriented. The yard resembles a huge basin. It is concave, and the cellar wall stands on a concrete base. From the very bottom, from a rat's perspective, you can't see the gap under the gate, the crumbled bricks in the side wall, the wide-open outlet of the rainwater pipe, you can't see any place where a rat could hide. I circle the yard, exploring every nook. From the middle of the yard, from the place where the little female rat perished, I see only the lids of the metal garbage cans and the iron pump against the background of the wall.

A muffled sound made by teeth grinding on a bone comes from the garbage can into which the little female rat was thrown.

I quickly climb the lid, which is open and hangs from the rim. I am hungry, constantly hungry.

The garbage can is filled with all sorts of refuse — empty

boxes, tin cans, paper, bones, banana and orange peels, rags, husks, hair, apple cores.

I eat a few crumbs of stale bread. I crawl deeper. The sounds of something being devoured are more distinct.

The little female should be somewhere here.

Lower and lower. At the bottom a large old rat is gobbling up the entrails of the little female rat. I approach cautiously. I hear the grinding of his powerful teeth. He allows me to stay. He sniffs me carefully, touches me with his whiskers, checks, examines. I do the same, ready at any moment to escape. Instead of attacking me, he lets me join him. The meat of the little female is tender and tasty.

We devour her, leaving the bones and the skin.

I am satisfied, full, heavy.

The old rat pushes his way to the surface through rustling paper. I follow him.

The moon shines over the yard. I stand on my hind paws, leaning on my tail, and raise my head. I stare long at the moon's bright surface. The old rat quenches his thirst with water dripping from the pump.

A noiseless shadow has eclipsed the surface of the moon. It hovers over us. It descends. The old rat flattens against the ground. I sense the danger and leap toward the garbage can. A huge owl brushes me with its wings.

It has large terrifying eyes and hooked claws. The old rat jumps; he is beside me. The night bird issues a shrill cry and rises into the air. For a while longer it hovers over the yard. It flies away.

In the street. I slink along the gutter in the shade of the curb, inhaling the smell of the cool, wet pavement.

The old rat clearly enjoys such wanderings. Time after time I touch the tip of his tail with my whiskers.

I try to remember the way: I want to return to my cellar.

The old rat runs across the street. I see people on the opposite sidewalk. The old rat ignores their presence; he is calm, confident, indifferent. He stops next to the curb, near people who are standing. His shape blends in with the street pavement, it disappears in it. The flagstones glisten in the glow of tall streetlights. Against this background the old rat's sheenless fur is almost invisible.

I follow him, I quickly slink across the street.

In the distance I notice light moving toward us. Screeching, whirring, roaring. The old rat shows no concern. He moves along the gutter as if he didn't see the increasing brightness, as if he didn't hear the noise, the roaring.

I squeeze under a greasy scrap of newspaper. Next to us a car equipped with strong headlights drives by with great speed.

The first car I have encountered on my way. I haven't had time to recover from fright when another one comes, and another, and still another. Half deaf, I creep out from under the paper. The cars are gone, the street is quiet. The old rat has hidden in a nook between the curb and the drain cover. Sitting on his hind paws, he devours a sausage skin that he has just found. Until now I wasn't aware of the delicacies gathered here — fatback, wet bread, a rotten banana, apple cores.

I feel hunger — quite a long time has passed since my last meal. I sit beside the old rat and keep on eating until my hunger is satisfied.

*   *   *

I am in the sewers. Time passes imperceptibly, like the black streams of sewage and refuse. From above — from the round manholes and drains covered with grates — dim light, similar to the light in our cellar, seeps in.

The old rat led me in here through the narrow crack between the iron rim of the drain and the flagstones.

Hollowed-out corridors run in all directions under the street, under the sidewalks and the pavement, going up and down, sloping gently and steeply, between the walls of the sewers and the ground, on many levels. A vast, intricate labyrinth inhabited by masses of rats stretches under tiles, floors, concrete slabs, under yards and garages, repair shops and cellars.

This whole world, my wonderful world, is consumed by an incessant fever to procure food, to gorge, devour, eat, tear to pieces, kill, bite, attack, to destroy the weaker one, the smaller one, the one who can't defend himself, who is different, alien, whose smell is intolerable.

Keeping by the old rat's side, I traverse the world, the world I sensed when I first set out on my way along the sewage pipe, the world I tried to reach by myself when I sought the possibility of leaving the nest.

And although I choke with fear when rats rushing in murderous pursuit run straight into me, or when I come across an alien rat that has been killed, I feel this is my place, my home, I am in my own element.

The old rat knows his way around the immense labyrinth. He follows routes known only to himself, routes that lead to destinations known only to himself.

He doesn't lead me but lets me follow him, he tolerates me beside or behind him. I found that out when I tried to overtake him. With all his strength he bit my tail right at the base, and if I hadn't backed away from him, he would most

21

likely have killed me. So with the bleeding tail I stayed behind him, his bent, powerful back before me.

I don't overtake him, I run after him, I yield to his will, I rely on him. . . .

A stream of sewage flows in a wide canal. The old rat is running along its edge. Suddenly he stops, bends over the water, submerges. The current carries him off; he floats. I plunge after him. Water floods my ears, eyes, and nostrils. It has a pleasant salty-sour taste, and it smells of watered-down urine. Instinctively I move my paws and swim. The head of the old rat stands out clearly against the ripples on the water.

Reaching the opposite side, he hooks his claws into the rough surface, he jumps out onto the bank. He shakes himself, and the flying drops of water hit my eyes.

I gather all my strength to resist the strong current pushing me toward the middle of the stream. I move my paws frantically, trying to hold my head high so that the waves won't fall on my face. I approach the opposite wall at almost exactly the same place as the old rat. I fasten the claws of my front and hind paws to the surface. I fail the first time, fall into the stream again. I drive my claws into the hollows, I tense my muscles. This time the jump is perfect. Water flows down my fur. I shake myself a few times. The old rat is already gone. I follow his tracks, which have been impressed into the moist layer that covers the floor. I find him around the corner, staring at a small gray ball that resembles a miniature rat.

A mouse is holding a big white worm in his mouth. The mouse raises his head and in this uncomfortable position walks forward. Preoccupied with his prey, he doesn't see us. He pulls, pushes, tosses the wiggling worm — in order to move ahead. At the place where dim light seeps in, he pulls his prey up over brick rubble.

I want to jump; the muscles in my back grow taut. As if he had anticipated my excitement, the old rat turns and touches my nostrils with his whiskers. In the meantime the mouse has reached his destination — a narrow crevice in the arched ceiling.

One leap, and the old rat freezes at the opening. I can hear soft squeaking from the bottom of the crevice.

Mice inhabit the corridor, which has been deserted by rats.

The noise suggests that there are many of them. The old rat runs inside. The corridor branches off. All the exits should be blocked so that no mouse can escape. We burst in. The mice are running away, hurling themselves at the walls, jumping over our backs.

The old rat bites murderously. A movement of the teeth is enough, and the mouse falls down with a torn throat, a crushed neck, or a broken spine.

I notice a female covering squeaking shapes with her body. Terrified, she holds in her teeth a young mouse. The little one moves its paws. A quick movement, and the female dies with her larynx bitten in two. I kill the little ones. With my teeth I tear the delicate pink meat, I swallow, I absorb.

My movements become perfect, more and more precise. Killing didn't come easily to me at the beginning. Killing the mouse or the bird required many redundant movements. Now the strikes are confident — I kill feeling almost no resistance.

The old rat keeps searching. On the opposite side he has sniffed a nest. Its entrance is concealed under scraps of newspaper. The squeaking confirms that he has found a large family of mice there.

From the exposed opening to the nest a male emerges, dragging behind him his paralyzed hind legs. I crush his neck.

The old rat hauls all the dead mice into one spot.

The teeth of the old rat have torn the mice into pieces. My teeth inflict no such wounds yet, work no such havoc.

Full of food, we leave the burrow. Strange rats wait at the entrance. They want to slip inside, lured by the smell of the blood.

The old rat passes them, indifferent.

We set out for the slaughterhouse, where we drink the still-warm blood, for the grain and flour warehouses, for the bakery, the dairy, the refuse containers and garbage receptacles, for the stables and the pigpens, farther and farther.

The old rat knows dumps and alleys. He foresees danger, he warns against the nests of wasps and bumblebees, against a stalking fox, a marten, and a weasel. He teaches me how to get honey out of a bottle that stands in the pantry — by biting out the cork and then dipping my tail in the bottle. He moves confidently, aware of the strength of his powerful, fast-growing teeth. With his teeth he pries the metal lid off a jar filled with aromatic lard, he bites through the tin cover of a can of meat, he cuts the strings on which smoked hams hang.

The old rat takes good care of his teeth. Through a dark tunnel that was dug out by rats, we are going toward the surface. I hear the distant rattling of a streetcar, the humming of a passing crowd. We are walking along a concrete surface. One of the slabs that lie close together has crumbled. We squeeze inside, careful not to cut our bellies on the uninsulated bars of the steel reinforcements. Heavy cables in lead casings cross the interior, which is padded with layers of tar paper and tar. Small shiny sparks flicker along the cables. I notice the marks of rats' teeth on them. The ground is covered with metal particles.

I bite, I spit out the pulverized lead. My jaws work rhythmically. The resistance of the metal infuriates me. I try to conquer it. I look for a better position and bite from different directions. The lead casing gives way. I cut the thin wires that are inside. The shiny sparks burn my gums. I quit. We go back.

Heavy, with gray thinned-out fur on his back and sides, scarred ears resembling frayed mushrooms, a long, hairless, broken tail that has no tip, the old rat has retained his slyness and agility, his strength and caution.

Staying with him, I observe his skills and adopt them. I learn to recognize danger, I learn to anticipate it. Cats, dogs, snakes, hawks, owls, crows, pigs' teeth, horses' hooves, cows' hooves and horns, traps, lead weights falling on the head, chicken and fish heads stuffed with poison, poisoned grains, caustic liquids and toxic gases pumped into the nests, people, and rats — the old rat knows all possible dangers. He has learned about them during his long life. He knows that a roaring car is less dangerous than an owl flying noiselessly or a cat walking softly.

Delicious-smelling pastries lie in the corner of the cellar. The old rat sniffs them, walks away, comes back, sniffs them again, without touching them with his teeth.

With great difficulty, trying not to touch the surface of the pastries with his fur, he sprays them with urine and leaves his droppings on them to signal that they are inedible.

There's nothing to eat among the piles of paper in the neighboring cellars. But in several places we discover pastries scattered like those we saw earlier. And in a nest located inside a crate full of paper, we find the dead bodies of a rat family that has gorged on those poisoned delicacies.

We also find many deserted nests from which rats have wandered away. We find decaying mice and a stiffened dead cat.

We quickly leave this building full of poisons. At another time I discover the appetizing head of a smoked cod impaled on a steel wire. The old rat acts as if the delicious smell hasn't reached him at all. That cools me off a little, although the sight of the fish head dripping fat tempts me so much that I swallow the mucus that has trickled into my throat.

The old rat continues on his way as if the fish head radiating delicious aromas isn't here. A cheerful young rat darts past us, lured by the smell.

In a moment he will crouch over the tasty prey, he will dig his incisors into the crunchy, fragrant skin. He will taste the delicate fibers, devour gelatinous eyes, and eat into the brain.

I'll take the fish head away from him. I am stronger. I turn back.

The head is still stuck on a hooked wire. The young rat approaches. A loud crash. A metal cylinder smashes the young rat's back. Blood trickles down his incisors. His tail quivers spasmodically. The end. I want to escape. The old rat darts straight to the fish head. Leaning on his tail, he lifts himself, pulls the fish head off the hooked wire. Holding it tight in his teeth, he comes back to me. The body of the young rat, with the smashed back and bloody mouth, is left in the trap. I follow the old rat, I follow the wonderful smell of the smoked fish.

The city has fewer and fewer secrets. I get to know it

thoroughly, house by house, street by street. I know where most cats come and where owls hunt most often, what a trap with a tasty-looking bait looks like, and how to avoid poisons. I also know that my fur is the most effective means of protection. Against the dark surface of the garbage dump, on the pavement, in the gutter, against the dirty-gray background of the street, I'm almost invisible. And this is your advantage in the eternal strife against danger, in the constant war with people.

The old rat belongs to no community of rats in my city, although he has spent a long time here, as is evidenced by his excellent knowledge of the area and his ability to find his way faultlessly in all the local labyrinths.

His smell has preserved its individual character — it's different from the smells of all the local rat families. Yet its strangeness never irritates or provokes attacks. I have found out that many times the kind of smell a rat gives off has determined his fate.

Each rat family recognizes its members by their own smell, peculiar only to them. Some families are exceptionally large — often a neighborhood, sometimes larger areas, even the whole city, belong to them. There are also families that consist of only a few members.

The appearance of a stranger arouses immediate excitement, and his alien smell causes anxiety. It is uncertain if the first one won't be followed by others, if they won't try to oust the local rats from their feeding ground and nests, if they won't drive them out or kill them.

The smell of a stranger indicates what his intentions are, whether he comes by himself or leads his family in search of new feeding grounds.

27

In most cases the strange rat is attacked at once by local rats. Sometimes the attack is feigned, serving only to drive the intruder out, but most commonly the stranger is killed and devoured.

Rats rarely accept a stranger into their family and allow him to build his own nest with a local female.

The old rat wanders, travels, moves from place to place. He doesn't build nests, he doesn't stay with any female permanently, doesn't raise young ones. He doesn't feel attachment to the labyrinths that he has come to know.

The well-known and explored places interest him no longer — they become unattractive and boring. What matters is the new, the unknown, what is before him. And so there's another city, a new system of cellars and sewers, other dangers, bewildering labyrinths.

The old rat isn't satisfied with peace, which most rats consider the basis of their existence — the cozy family nest, the familiar cellar, the full pantry. Rats like a settled way of life, in a labyrinth they have come to know, without insecurity, changeability, dangers. Here they always know where to look for food and what food can be found at what time. Local dangers are also familiar: traps in more or less the same places, lazy cats stretching in the sunny yards, owls flying at dusk, the same people. Nothing unusual, no surprises. Such a life seems to most rats safer, easier, ensuring more chances of survival.

But not all rats find such a life appealing. Some leave their families, their cellars, the old paths that have been trod on by generations. These rats set out for the unknown. Most of those journeys end in untimely death — almost the moment the rat leaves the familiar territory. Only the most intelligent rats acquire experience and reach old age.

It's most difficult to abandon one's own nest, one's own cellar, one's past life.

The later stage comes with leaving the family circle. This first expedition, often the last one, may end with the terrified young rat's return to the family nest, or it may become a stage in his further travels, in his later attempts to wander.

I follow him, watching intently the dusk that surrounds us in the cellar. The old rat stops and begins prolonged grooming. I squat on my hind paws by the wall and start cleaning my fur.

The old rat is skilled in catching fleas. Time and again I hear his teeth snap. He hunts fleas with a vengeance. First, using his claws, he drives them from his back, head, and neck into a more accessible place, only to bend over later and destroy them one by one with his teeth. Unfortunately, I am no match for him in those activities. Fleas run away from under my nose, they move faster than I can catch them. I snap my teeth in vain. With great difficulty I catch only a few. The old rat suddenly stops cleaning his long whiskers.

He sniffs, looks around. I pay no attention to him. I wash myself with my own saliva, licking dirt off the surface of my fur. I moisten my paws, I wipe my eyes and nostrils.

The old rat's back grows taut, his hair bristles, signaling danger.

The cellar seems pleasant, warm and cozy.

I stop washing and look around suspiciously. A short distance away, right beside the wall, I notice two gleaming eyes. It's a cat.

We have run away from cats many times. But no cat has

ever been so close. His eyes glow more brightly now. He is readying himself to spring.

There's no place to escape to. All the doors are covered with thick metal. Not even the smallest chink through which I could squeeze. The cement floor is smooth, with no opening, no drain. The spots where gas and water pipes are set into the wall are covered with a fresh layer of oil paint.

The small window in the back of the corridor has two windowpanes and closely spaced iron bars.

We are trapped. The only way out — the way of return — is blocked by the cat's glowing eyes. The angle of his gaze tells me that he is staring at the old rat.

Controlling his fear, slowly, as if nothing threatened us, the old rat moves toward the opposite wall. The glowing eyes follow him watchfully. Suddenly the old rat hurls himself straight at the barred window. He leaps high and with his claws clings to the metal grating. The cat follows him and runs close to me. I can clearly see his sharp white teeth and drawn-out claws. If he springs on me, I will perish. He doesn't.

The old rat has aroused exceptional hatred in him.

I run away.

The cat leaps up. The old rat with all his strength bounces off the metal grating, springs toward the ceiling. He pushes himself off the smooth surface and falls on the back of the raging cat. A moment of whirling, meowing, squeaking.

The old rat jumps toward the wall again. The cat jumps after him. But the old rat has gained an advantage: he has a way to escape, and what's more, the cat is no longer certain of his strength.

The old rat is running in my direction. He jumps down the stairs to an almost identical corridor located on a lower level. Only this window has no dense grating, and its broken windowpane allows you to go through it onto the low, flat roof. The old rat runs right behind me, the cat behind him. I slide down the wall, which is overgrown with vines, and rush into the haven of a rats' burrow.

On the roof, the old rat stops, turns, shows his powerful teeth. The cat stops, hisses, meows furiously.

The old rat's ears are bloodied — the claws must have reached him. The cat's nostrils are torn, and one of his eyes is half shut. The adversaries threaten each other, afraid to engage in the final clash. The old rat suddenly issues a sharp squeak, as if he wanted to attack the cat. The cat retreats abruptly, and the old rat jumps off the edge of the roof into the chink between the eaves and the wall.

After a while he touches me with his bloodied whiskers. Only now do I see that the cat has clawed the skin on the rat's back, ripped his ear, and hurt his eye. Along a pipe corroded by rust, we reach the familiar snug tunnels. The old rat begins long, meticulous grooming. I sniff him carefully. His hair has retained the smell of the cat's paws. I lick off a drop of blood that has congealed on his torn ear.

Because he is afraid of a sudden attack and fury, the old rat avoids entering inhabited rats' nests.

Unpleasant memories of situations in which he barely avoided death must hold him back. He also avoids places with only one entrance. Even if, running away from a cat, an owl, or a weasel, we find shelter in such a place, he always displays unusual nervousness and leaves the unsafe place the moment the danger is over.

It's later, after my own experiences, that I get to know the causes of that fear.

The old rat has no nest of his own and never tries to start

31

one. His attitude toward female rats is also atypical. In fact, he should give up the idea of copulation, since rats his age feel no sexual urge. But the old rat's behavior contradicts this rule.

We rats form couples, and each partner is deeply jealous of the other, although I have encountered families in which all females copulated with all males. Males for the most part are more jealous, and they drive out any intruder that comes near their female.

This mainly applies to females in heat, which are well-disposed toward all males that come up to them.

The appearance of the old rat causes major turmoil in the world of those rules. It often ends in fights, in which I sometimes participate.

The fights conclude with the settled local rats driving the old rat out into another tunnel or into the cellars of the neighboring building. So the old rat approaches females only when their males aren't nearby.

I am an adult male, and when the old rat dismounts a female, I try at once to take his place. More often than not I am successful, although some females won't let me come near or will bite me and push me away with their hind paws.

Earlier I had sex only with the little female in the nest, and I had no suitable experience. Now I feel the need to have a female permanently, but staying with the old rat, I am forced to have only casual encounters, which often end in my escape through cellars, sewers, and garbage dumps.

Now and then — when his attempts to gain the favor of a female fail — the old rat mounts my back, holds the skin on my back with his teeth, squeezes my sides hard with his paws, and in that way satisfies his sexual urges. I dislike playing the role of a female, the more so that when I once tried to reverse the roles, he threw me off his back and bit me badly.

Local males who at first tolerated the old rat have become suspicious and often aggressive now that he has started copulating with their females. Several times he has come close to being torn to pieces by raging groups of rats that hold him at bay. Although I stay with the old rat all the time, my smell is so familiar and recognizable that the local rats choose not to attack me yet. But the old rat, discouraged because of his failures and difficulties, more and more frequently clasps my back with his paws, and satisfying his needs, he passes his smell on to me.

I recognize my father among the rats attacking the old rat. I recognize him from a distance because at one time his front paw was broken and he limps.

He attacks the old rat together with the other rats, agitated at the appearance of a stranger.

The pursuit, in which I also participate, lasts briefly. The old rat turns and with his teeth grabs the throat of the male that is right behind him. He tears the rat's throat in a flash. At the same time Father bites me on the back, close to my ear.

I spring at his throat, and with a few movements of my incisors, I deeply cut his neck. He tries to defend himself against further bites, but he has no strength left. He is dying. The convulsive movements of his tail and paws indicate that the end is coming. Blood trickles down his incisors. The other rats run away in panic.

The old rat sniffs the dead body and begins his usual grooming. After a moment he stops, runs to me, and jumps on my back.

*　　　*　　　*

The old rat runs nervously all over the town. He doesn't stay very long anywhere. It's as if a dangerous, unknown enemy is pursuing him and tracking him.

I know that the old rat has begun to view the city as a strange and hostile territory. Until now it has been solely a stage — maybe a somewhat longer stopover — in his journey.

But now he suddenly feels threatened, surrounded by well-known gates, sewers, and cellars full of rats who hate him. The city, which quite recently he was still discovering, now irritates and bores him. And although he stays here out of his own will, he is now convinced that it is the city that detains him and prevents him from wandering farther.

The old rat has experienced such situations many times, and that is exactly why he has never settled anywhere, never stayed anywhere for good. He now attacks all the rats he encounters. He even attacks a young cat, which runs away terrified.

He is left with hate only, hate for everything he finds in the city, hate that is feverish, violent, unpredictable, hate that has to be relieved.

Running pell-mell through the neighborhoods, the old rat doesn't hide in cellars and sewers as before. On the contrary: he disregards danger, he slips past people terrified at the sight of him, often close to the wheels of cars. It is not a disregard for danger but simply an indifference to every-thing unrelated to his main goal. And his only goal is to leave the city as soon as possible.

He feels trapped, surrounded, locked up — even though the area in which he moves is large enough for the local rats to live in.

He visits railroad stations, bridges, overpasses, loading docks, warehouses. For some time he circles the cargo sheds of a river port.

34

It seems that he can't decide how and when to leave the city.

Sniffing crates, packages, sacks, freight cars, and baggage becomes his daily activity. He searches for the dependable smell, the smell that will calm him, the odor that he can trust, that will let him rest and leave.

This daily search didn't last long.

On a railroad loading dock where we go every day, the old rat carefully sniffs a pile of grain-filled sacks ready for loading. There are many piles, and he sniffs them one by one. All those actions, which make no sense to me at the time, bore and vex me.

Recently the old rat's attitude toward me has also changed drastically. He often bites and claws me, he turns me over and nips my belly, causing me a lot of pain. More than once I run away from him because he gives the impression that he wants to bite me to death. He runs after me, squeaking shrilly.

In his hatred for the city he must have decided that I have stopped him, imprisoned him. And since I always accompany him and am constantly nearby, he vents his bitterness and fury on me.

I was scared, I was growing more and more scared.

But although he keeps driving me away more and more relentlessly, I don't want to desert him. When, during one of the attacks, he turns me over onto my back and with all his strength bites my neck, I take advantage of the situation and with a fast movement of my teeth I rip his ear.

I wrench myself free and escape.

Staying as close to him as before, I risk death at any moment. I decide to go away, to leave him by himself. Maybe he expects that. He simply is fed up with my constant presence.

I want to leave and I can't. I follow his route, I follow his tracks, I keep circling him.

And now I am watching his excited movements from a short distance: nervous sniffing of the stacks of canvas sacks, standing on his hind paws, moving his whiskers as if in fear of danger. At last he finds the smell he has been looking for, the smell that gives a sense of security to the new journey for which he yearns. Suddenly he climbs up and disappears among the piled-up gray shapes. He has found the place he was seeking. Most likely he has bitten a hole in the canvas. People are hanging lines, attaching them to a suspended steel hook. The lifted load rocks in the huge gate of the crane that is moving on the rails.

I start missing the old rat after he leaves the city. Until now I walked behind him, I saw his bony back, his long, scaly tail.

He chose the route, he decided which way was the shortest, the safest, the surest. He led.

Running on the slippery edge of the sewer, I search for him now. I search for him, knowing that he has wandered away, that he has escaped the city. I search for him, even though in my memory I carry the image of the tall frame of a receding crane and the rocking load of sacks filled with grain, among which he hid. I saw that but still I search, knowing that finding him is impossible. I search because I want to ease my anxiety, control the nervous shivering of my body, return to the rat's ordinary life. I search to convince myself that searching will change nothing.

In the sewer I kill and devour a mouse, in the garbage dump I find the leftover remains of pig's meat, at dusk I scour the gutter and the streets downtown.

A noiseless shadow flies high above. It cuts across the

sharp light of the streetlamp. An owl. I hide at once in the darkness of the sewage drain. I wait for the shadow to fly away. That's right, I am close to the cellar in which I was born. I cross the sidewalk and reach the tall iron gate. I return to the paved yard of the bakery where I met the old rat. I jump onto the ledge of the cellar window with ease. The stack of bricks and boxes is here, just as it was before. But the sewage pipes are covered with fresh paint, which has an unpleasant odor.

I smell my family. I find rat droppings everywhere. Through a chink I get into the cellar. Hazy light falls in through the window — the reflection of the streetlight. Here, between the faucet and a pile of coal covered with boards, I find the entrance to my nest, my burrow. The familiar family smell assaults my nostrils, stuns, summons. I run along the short corridor.

A large female, my mother, is resting among young rats and chewing a bread crust.

Her hair bristles at the sight of me. Showing her strong incisors, she shields the young rats with her body. I withdraw quickly. She follows me; I can feel her whiskers touch my tail.

I stop at the faucet and turn. Our whiskers touch. We sniff each other's bodies. I smell a strong exciting odor that is secreted by all females in heat. I feel a violent urge to copulate. I lick off the liquid trickling down her belly.

She stiffens, clings to the ground, raises her tail, exposing the opening wet with mucus. She squeaks shrilly. I mount her, clasp her sides with my paws, hold the skin on her back with my teeth. At climax I squeak loudly.

She crawls around with her tail raised, she lures, provokes, excites. One more time we satisfy our needs. She goes back to the burrow. When I try to follow her into it, she turns and lightly bites me on the ear. She warns me not to move farther. She is concerned about the young rats I might kill.

I have my own nest, my own female — my own mother, whom I will repeatedly inseminate — my own family. I also have my own hunting ground, which is scattered with my droppings, and my own area for procuring food. I am an adult rat who knows dangers and enemies, who knows his way around perfectly, who is shrewd and sly, strong and cautious.

But the location of our burrow worries me. Its only exit lies in an open space right behind the elbow joint of the faucet. The moment this exit is shut, we will be cut off. There's no other way out of the nest.

The old rat taught me to avoid similarly built nests.

He carefully examined each location he found himself in, and if it aroused his suspicions, he left it at once.

But I don't want to leave the burrow. I don't want to go away from the cozy cellar of the bakery, where a lot of food can be found without difficulty. I don't want to give up living in the place where I was born, where the smell of our family permeates each corner. If I hadn't returned here, my fate could have taken a different turn.

I can no longer leave. The mother-female is pregnant again, and at the same time she is raising the earlier litter. The young ones frolic all over the cellar and, squeaking, run out into the corridor. Looking at them, I recall my own first wanderings and the curiosity that drove me into the unknown.

What happened to the rats from that litter? I know only the fate of the little female. I can guess the fate of the others.

Fewer and fewer young rats come back from their sallies out of the burrow.

The first one was caught by a cat lounging on sunny days on the balcony right over the yard. The next one was crushed by the door, which was opened suddenly.

The young females wandered along the cellar corridor, across the yard, all the way to the street, and never came back. The last male was squashed by the steel arm of the trap.

The mother accompanies me on my trips, along the gutters, to the nearby sewers and cellars.

During those forays, time and again we come upon deserted rats' nests to which I would gladly move. I am most interested in the attic of a neighboring house, which is above an empty apartment.

Winter is coming, and the first colder night drives us out of the attic, back into our warm cellar in the back of the old bakery.

Settling in the sewers — which seem safest — doesn't suit my female either. I notice that she has a deadly fear of water, and if she happens to get into it, that is only through an oversight — when she jumps or falls after slipping on the edge of the sewer. Each such occurrence causes an attack of fury, which for the most part she wreaks on me.

She goes back to the cellar under the bakery and won't leave it for a long time.

Such trips are possible only when the mother has already raised her little ones but the next pregnancy doesn't yet impede her movements.

Her fear of water is inexplicable. Swimming in the sewers in all directions, with the current, against the current, the old rat felt no fear of water. On the contrary, he used the current in swimming where he wanted to go. I learned that during our wanderings together.

The female's fear of the smallest underground stream or even of rainwater flowing into a street drain irritates me.

So we live in a snug cellar under the bakery, in the dim light seeping in through the window, in unchanging cozy warmth, in an interior without gusts of wind.

I try to dig a tunnel from our nest to the neighboring cellar, but each time I encounter a hard wall covered with a layer of tar that a rat's teeth can't gnaw through. The foundation of the neighboring house has a solid concrete base.

I try to bore downward. Maybe I'll encounter the sewer wall, the casing of sewage pipes or of telephone cables, and find in them a suitable fissure. Our nest would then have another exit. I dig and rake the soil out with my paws. The ground consists of pieces of plaster, fragments of moldered bricks, and wood ashes. Apparently, the building that used to stand here has burned. I keep listening for the distant murmur of water, but I can't hear anything. I don't come upon a sewer. After several consecutive attempts, I reach the old wall, made of large, sound bricks.

The wall stops me.

I can still go upward. Maybe I'll find crevices that lead outside or cracks in the walls.

That also fails. I encounter steel girders supporting the cellar ceiling. So our nest is surrounded by walls, and it's impossible to break out.

Successive generations of rats come into the world. They are born, they grow, they leave, are born, grow, leave. The cycle repeats itself many times, regardless of the season. The majority of those rats perish during the first weeks of their independence.

While the mother feeds them, I search for food. More and more frequently I steal into the storage rooms of the bakery. I discover a convenient way there through a broken wall fan. I go through it carrying pieces of bread, cake, various fruits, cheese, fatback. I often return, my fur smeared with lard, butter, frosting, or sprinkled with flour. Then the whole family licks the food off my fur. Again and again I loot the storeroom. I gnaw through a large box filled with sweet powdered sugar. That is a rare delicacy, although I prefer lump sugar, which is excellent for the incisors. I return to the nest covered with sweet powder. The female and the little ones lick my every hair.

A few times I wander to the storeroom with the young rats.

The sight of so much food rids them of all fear. They forget about everything. That is why, when they come here by themselves, they will fall prey to a lurking cat, or, lured by the smell, they will fall into traps with a smoked fish head. A rat mustn't forget dangers; a rat's life is constantly threatened. He is besieged from all sides.

The young rats are merry, playful, trusting, and curious about everything around them. They are interested in a patch of light, the movement of a leaf, an unfamiliar chink in the wall, an insect running across the wall. They are fascinated by life, by its variety and richness, by the possibilities it offers, the roads that open in all directions.

A torn mouse, a slain sparrow, a fish skeleton with the remains of meat on the bones — those surrounding proofs of death fail to make an impression. The rats don't associate them with their everyday life, which is joyous, full of jumps and falls, feigned attacks and chases.

We hold them back and protect them as long as it's possible. But the mother already feels a new litter growing inside. She stops taking care of the young rats, lets them make solitary excursions farther and farther. The next litter will require protection, and the nest has to be ready to receive them.

The young rats leave. Curiosity carries them forward, ahead, on the road toward discovery.

We, the adult rats, fear lighted, bright spaces, where foes lurk all around. Totally blind a while ago, the young rats don't associate any unpleasant memories with light. Just the opposite: when a light bulb is burning in the cellar and traces of light reach their still-closed eyelids, they strive toward it.

Likewise, later, when their lids separate and the young rats see for the first time the dark interior of the nest, they will crawl stubbornly to the lighted contour of the exit.

From there unknown noises and smells reach them, from there I bring them food. Therefore they have to get there with the utmost haste, to get to know the bright, shiny, dazzling, colorful reality.

The little rats crawl out. The mother wants to stop them, she grabs them by their skin and carries them back. They squeak with powerless anger. They will make their first trips with the mother or with me.

In the neighboring cellar there's a chink next to the sewage pipe. I use it to crawl under the big oven. The stuffiness and heat here cause the fleas to leave my fur in droves.

The bakery building, old and crumbling, has been renovated many times, and some of the chinks have been filled with plaster. Right here in the wall, near which stands a huge kneading trough, I discover such a plaster-filled hole behind the steadily humming metal device that is installed high above the ground. From the opening I jump onto a tall cupboard, and from there onto the floor, close to the door of the storeroom. In the door, or, to be more exact, between the doorframe and the wall, I find a place with a missing wooden knot. When there are no people in the bakery, I widen the opening enough for me to squeeze through it easily.

That way, by going through the broken fan or taking a much shorter way through the bakery, I can visit the storeroom. It's true the way through the bakery is much more dangerous, but it doesn't require going outside. But to get to the fan I have to come from the old shed. Its slanting cornice lies next to the water pipe that runs above the paved yard.

To cross the bakery I use the dark strip of ceramic tiles that surrounds the floor. Hampers with dirty aprons, tin baking molds, pots for mixing flour, stand there for the most part.

Busy with work, the people don't have time to look around. The mother knows only the route through the fan. Now I show her the much shorter way that doesn't require climbing the water pipe, which is sometimes wet and at other times covered by ice. As it turns out, this route isn't always accessible to her. The unsurmountable obstacle is her swollen pregnant belly, which makes it impossible for her to push through the narrow chink in the doorframe. So the mother goes that way only after she gives birth to another litter and as long as the size of her belly allows.

On the table in the middle of the storeroom I discover a box filled with eggs, rats' greatest delicacy.

At one time the old rat and I went to the henhouse, and there I tasted an egg for the first time. Lying in the dark, the oval shape resembled a stone. The old rat sniffed it first, then he encircled the egg with his tail and moved it to a hole that he had gnawed in a wooden board. There, with his incisors, he cut a small opening in the egg and began to lick the flowing white. Later he enlarged the opening, and at last he split the egg into two parts. He left behind a completely cleaned out shell.

The smell of the egg yolk being eaten filled the room and whetted my appetite so much that I pounced on the first egg I found in the henhouse.

The hard surface initially resisted my incisors. Finally I struck the eggshell from above and made a small opening in it.

Inside I found no yolk, only a half-grown chicken floating in tasty, nice-smelling liquid.

My eating was interrupted by a furious, loudly cackling hen, which circled me and wanted to peck out my eyes. I was trying to chase her away when a rooster appeared. He was running toward me with an outstretched neck and a bulging comb. I escaped. Later I often stole with the old rat into henhouses, pantries, stores.

I learned to wrap my tail around the egg and drag it behind me. Now, in the bakery storeroom, I can savor the taste of egg yolks at will.

After satisfying my own hunger, I decide to roll an egg to the nest.

Yet my tail is too weak to move the eggs lying in enclosures.

I raise the egg with my nose and remove it with my paws from the hollow in which it is resting. It doesn't stop on the table but falls with a loud crash. The sound scares me so much that I hide in the broken fan. After a while I run down to where a broken egg is lying on the floor. Only then do I realize that an egg can't be rolled from the storeroom to the nest.

But that doesn't keep us from further attempts at removing eggs from their cardboard boxes. Together with the mother, I eat several that night and break many more.

I set off for the storeroom with two young ones. They follow me across the bakery, empty at that time. They are jumping, squeaking, tumbling.

We begin to feast. The bellies become rounder. We have to go back. Soon people will come, and then returning will be difficult. I won't risk going back through the fan, along the snow-covered cornice or the frozen water pipe. Hungry owls hover over neighboring yards all night long.

Meanwhile one of the little ones finds a trap with the head of a smoked fish in the corner of the storeroom. There are more and more such traps. They stand on the stairs, in the cellars, in the attic, in the yard.

They are constructed in such a way that a rat doesn't die at once. The lead weight usually hits him in the loin area, shattering his pelvis and spine. Crushed, he dies slowly, unable to wrench himself free. Pain often makes him gnaw his own paws.

The little rat becomes literally flattened out on the board. Stunned by the pain, he clenches his teeth on the aromatic scales of the fish and tries to get up.

He doesn't comprehend his situation and doesn't quite know what has happened. He squeaks. Blood trickles down his teeth and from his ears. He claws the board.

The other little rat and I run away. In a moment people will come. We are already in the bakery. I feel the little one's whiskers on my tail. We come to the cupboard.

Instead of climbing the usual way, between the cupboard and the wall, the little rat goes farther. He runs along the pipe to the table, and from there he jumps onto the rim of a huge trough full of sweet, fragrant dough.

From the top of the cupboard I watch him tottering on its edge, maintaining balance with his tail. The sweet dough clings to his mouth. There's movement in the yard. The steps are approaching. The key makes a grinding noise in the lock. The little rat suddenly staggers. He leans his paws against the porous surface, falls in, moves desperately, submerging deeper and deeper. Only the dark quivering tail protrudes above the surface.

There's no trace of the little rat. The dough in that spot is slightly depressed.

People come in. When they switch the light on, I hear steady humming from the appliance that screens the hole I have made.

I continue my attempts to dig out a tunnel that will lead outside. The mother and the young ones also climb the sloping wall and gnaw it. A trickle of sand pours out of the hole, straight into our nostrils. If we keep on widening the hole, we will bury the whole nest under the sand.

Only one young female has survived from several consecutive litters. She is cautious, sly, fearful, alert. In a few leaps she quickly crosses open spaces. She stops and looks around to see if there is danger. She avoids lighted and bright places where she can be seen from a distance. She is scared, she is permanently scared. This fear lets her survive among enemies, survive and fight for her life.

My two females live then in the nest. The old female often rolls the young one over and bites her, trying to drive her away. The young one escapes but comes back after a while as if nothing had happened.

Feeding her young ones, the mother intently watches the other female as if she is a useless intruder. The young female builds her own nest in one of the tunnels that we dug out while looking for another exit.

She has chosen a spot at the end of the tunnel, close to the wall where a brick has crumbled out. Now she widens it, tramples it, uses her droppings to harden the ground, cushions her lair.

She brings shreds of paper, scraps of linen and wool, pieces of cotton wool, feathers, threads, any soft, fluffy, warm fabrics.

She prepares herself to give birth. Both sides of her back have thickened visibly. When she passes the mother or tries to approach her, the mother bares her sharp yellow incisors, and her hair bristles as if she were ready to attack. The young female escapes hurriedly and hides in the scraps of newspaper at the end of her tunnel.

The time of birth is coming. The young female leaves her den less and less frequently.

I return to the nest. Faint squeaking reaches me from the tunnel. The young female is lying among paper scraps. Blind and hairless, little rats suck her teats, swollen with milk. She lets me come near her and the little ones. I sniff them carefully. They need food. Until now the young female has been searching for food together with me. But now it's impossible. She has to watch the little ones.

The mother's young rats can already see. They scatter all over the nest. They learn to eat by themselves, to bite, to kill. Recently I brought them a live mouse, which they immediately tore to pieces.

From the storeroom I'm bringing the young female a piece of cheese.

I am already in the nest. I am about to turn to the entrance of the tunnel, when the old female snatches the cheese away.

The situation repeats itself, yet when the famished young female comes out of the tunnel and catches a few crumbs, she is severely bitten.

Only once do I manage to bring the young female an aromatic fish skin. Thirst bothers her most. The last time she drank was before birth. There is a small well with a tin cover, under which it is easy to squeeze. But the young female is afraid to leave the little ones. She tries to lick the moisture off the crumbled bricks or to suck the lumps of earth.

But she has to go out and get food. Otherwise she won't have milk. She is waiting for the right moment. The old female falls asleep. The young one slips out of the burrow, runs under the well cover, and drinks. She devours a few millipedes, which under normal circumstances she wouldn't touch.

The little ones are growing. Their pink skin sprouts a delicate gray fuzz, and the dark patches of eyes begin to show under the lids. The little rats are more active and aim unerringly for the milk-filled teats.

They need much more milk now than right after birth, and the young female feels hungry more and more often. She eats scraps of wool and cotton wool, chews paper, pounces on any insect that appears in the burrow. But hunger becomes difficult to endure, the more so that the old female is vigilant and won't allow me to bring even crumbs of food to the young female.

Only when the old female is asleep can the young female procure a few unfinished fish bones and a rancid piece of fatback.

Irritated by hunger, the young female decides at last to make a trip to the bakery. Otherwise the little rats will starve to death.

When she leaves the nest, the old female is asleep. But she wakes up soon. At once she rushes into the tunnel and one by one carries the little ones into the nest. She throws them among her own active rats.

From the opposite wall I watch a lesson in killing.

The mother kills one of the little rats and eats him. The young rats kill the others.

When the young female returns, dragging a dry bread crust that she pulled out of the garbage can, the little rats are already dead. First she looks for them in the tunnel, then she dashes into the nest, collects the half-eaten trunks, and tries to take them back. The old female jumps at her, turns her over, and bites her.

The young female finally manages to grasp the headless body of one of her little rats and hide it in her own nest.

Another birth awaits the young female soon. She leaves the nest and moves to the cellar on the opposite side. Dusty shelves stand here, broken crates lie around. People haven't come in here for a long time.

The young female builds her nest in a moth-eaten armchair that rests in the corner. The armchair seems an exceptionally secure and quiet place. But the most important thing is that water drips all the time from a nearby pipe. Again she collects papers, rags, and feathers, and she painstakingly stuffs the nest with them. She also hoards food: dry scraps of meat, fish heads, bread crusts.

I have two nests now. The old one, with the old female and the generation of rats about to reach maturity, and the new nest inside the armchair, where the young female is getting ready to have another litter.

Both nests are unsafe, and maybe that's why I seldom stay

49

in them, why I devote a lot of time to roaming. I get as far as the loading dock on which I saw the old rat for the last time.

Outside the city, in brick buildings next to the river, people raise pigs, a lot of huge pigs.

We city rats come here often. Some time ago this area belonged to a different family of rats — smaller, brown and black, of a more delicate, slender build, with dark hairs covering their tails.

They retreat. We destroy their nests, try to drive them out. Finally they get out, leaving an open field.

Running on the edge of a feeding or drinking trough, you have to be exceptionally careful. The most trivial stumble and fall, and the pig's mouth will devour you, crush you, ingest you. The pigs attack, chase, pursue. Their hooves and teeth are formidable, so I try to stay close to a hiding place: the fence, the ledge of the wall, the burrow, under the tin trough.

The smell of pig's meat fills my nostrils. The fodder in the troughs is generally pretty monotonous. It is the moving rolls of fat that keep provoking me. I choose the largest, heavy, immobile pig. I climb his back from behind, I bite through his skin and begin to eat.

The pig squeals, groans, tosses himself between the walls of the narrow enclosure that hinders his movements. He tries unsuccessfully to turn over onto his back, to shake me off, to crush me. He kicks, pushes both flanks against the walls. I dig my claws into his back and bite into the delicious, warm, pulsating, bloodied fatback. Warm blood is flowing down the skin.

The pig is still struggling to throw me off. I change my position and bite near the tail. The pig grunts, groans, rages.

It takes long. Tired from struggling, he lies down and now and then kicks with his too short legs.

Clumsy, fat, heavy, squeezed in between the boards of the enclosure, he becomes my prey. He howls, snorts, squeals, waiting for me to satisfy my hunger and go away. Suddenly the door to the pigpen opens, and a man runs toward us. With my teeth I tear out the last piece of fatback and escape. I go back the next night. The pig is gone. I pick out another one, equally heavy and clumsy. But here the enclosure is wider. The pig rolls over onto his back and almost squashes me.

I spring onto his head and bite his neck. He hits his head on the iron railing. I give up. I move to another building, full of fair young pigs. On my tail I feel the whiskers of the rat that inhabits the cellar on the other side of the bakery.

The young pigs are spirited and nervous. They sense our presence. They squeak, leap, kick, try to snap.

Their teeth are already sharp, their hooves hard. We seek one that is asleep, weakened, or sick. There. He lies on his side, now and again kicking with his hind leg. We come as close as possible.

My neighbor rat finds the place where the artery pulsates. He bites. The young pig springs to his feet, squeaks. The rat hangs at the pig's neck. I hurl myself at the pig from the other side. He strikes me with his foot and shoves me off. I jump on his back, dig my teeth in close behind the ear. He throws me off. We attack him from all sides. Covered with blood, squeaking, he runs around the railing. I jump at his throat. I cut the artery. He falls.

The smell of blood disperses far. Terrified piglets run around, squeaking.

Other rats gather. At first we try to drive them away, but there are more and more of them.

The young pig is still kicking and grunting. Suddenly the light comes on. The pigs clamor more loudly. People are approaching.

I go back. In the cellar I hear barking from the storeroom. It is fierce, furious, vicious. A while ago, in the street, a dog chased me to the gutter. If, risking my life, I hadn't jumped down through the grating, he would have shattered my spine. Barking upsets me, disturbs me, reminds me of that pursuit.

A strange rat hangs around the young female. I want to expel him, but he has already made himself feel at home inside the armchair and holds his ground. I head therefore to the old nest, where the old female, who is in heat, waits.

A lot has changed in the bakery and the cellars during my absence. The storeroom has been repainted, the rotten doorframe replaced, and even the smallest chink filled up.

The door from the bakery under which I used to sneak has been reinforced with an extra slat and covered with metal. All the holes in the walls of the bakery and the storeroom, as well as the chink behind the electric meter, have been sealed with cement. The pots, troughs, pans, and grills have been pushed away from the walls, making safe passage impossible.

The fan that was broken is whirring now, blocking the last access to the pantry.

In several places I discover newly installed traps.

Poisoned wheat lies scattered in the garbage and in the cellar. Taking advantage of the mother's inattention, the young rats crawl out of the burrow and eat the grain on the first day. I pass their stiffened bodies in different places.

Before long a trap kills the young rat who wanted to take my place in the old armchair.

What upsets me most is that every night people lock an

old cat in the cellar. This is the same cat that until now has been lounging on the balcony. Irritated, he prowls, meowing shrilly. At daybreak he catches a rat that came in through the half-opened window. In the morning, blind in one eye and with his spine broken, the rat is still alive. People throw him into a bucket full of water.

The cat senses our presence. He keeps a long watch next to the faucet and tries to stick his paw into the burrow. He also detects the young female and her litter in the armchair. He is unable to get to them. He only overturns a few jars and hurts his paws on the broken glass.

People often come to the cellar. They gesticulate, point to the holes and chinks in the wall. I sense danger, the impending catastrophe. People seal all openings, cracks, and crevices in the walls around the yard. I find out that they are doing the same thing in all the buildings adjacent to the bakery, as well as in the houses on the other side of the street.

They are led by a dog with a long pointed nose, always sniffing and barking at each scent.

I am sitting in the old armchair, bent over a piece of sinewy meat that I have brought from the garbage can.

The barking of the dog and the whistling sound of the air that he draws into his nose arouse fear in the young female. With her teeth she picks up the little ones and crawls over them, covers them with her whole body.

I leap out of the armchair, and by racing along the top shelf I reach the metal lampshade with a burning light bulb underneath. People enter. The dog leads them straight to the armchair. I flatten myself against the metal plate heated from below.

People remove the jars, push the shelves and boards away. They grab the armchair and carry it into the corridor. The infuriated dog sticks his head among the springs.

Violent scuffling, furious yelping, horrible squealing. Holding the hairless little rats in her mouth, the young female tries to escape. The dog seizes her, roughs her up, lifts her. The people pet him. They shake the hairless, squeaking litter out of the armchair and trample them with their heels.

They carry the armchair into the yard.

The metal plate with the bulb burning underneath gets increasingly hotter. The surface burns my paws, scorches my belly. I jump off. I run along the shelves to the window that opens onto the bright street full of cars.

I run along the wall toward the gutter. A man steps back abruptly, screams, points. I squeeze through the grated opening of the drain. A shimmering stream murmurs deep inside. I hesitate, I try to stop on the curved surface of the cover. I lose my balance. I jump.

I return. I cautiously slip into the cellar. The cat is gone; I can smell that he is no longer here. The armchairs, the shelves, and the old furniture have been moved away from the walls. The holes have been cemented. I go to the cellar where the old female's nest is. All the walls have been uncovered here as well. The coal has been shoveled into the middle of the room.

I look for the hole behind the faucet. It isn't here. The wall is wet, damp, smooth.

I inspect the whole cellar, check each corner. The hole was there behind the faucet.

I return, stop at the wall. I listen to every noise coming from behind the thick layer of cement. After a moment, as if from a great distance, I hear quiet scraping. The mother in vain tries to get out, to gnaw through the wall. Immured in the space that has no other exit, terrified, antic-ipating death, she will gnaw till the last moment of her life. There are still three young rats in the burrow. The mother will kill them out of hunger, out of thirst, out of powerless-ness.

She will drink their blood, eat their flesh. This will suffice for a little while. During that time she will gnaw through less than half a brick if she continues gnawing in one spot only. The sound of teeth grinding on the cement-and-brick surface will keep growing weaker until it dies out com-pletely.

I circle the bakery, I go to the empty cellars, I touch the cemented openings with my whiskers. There's silence, deep silence behind the wall. Not too long ago I listened to the muffled sound of teeth scraping on the wall. I began to gnaw from this side, behind the faucet, in the place where the entrance to the burrow was.

That must have awakened hope in the mother, because the echo coming from behind the wall had become quicker and stronger.

The cat frightened me away, and I didn't come back until the following night. The sounds from the other side had grown faint. The mother had lost her strength, her incisors had been worn down to her gums.

In vain, I begin to gnaw. My teeth barely scratch the cement surface.

I keep gnawing, even though not a sound comes from the other side. I gnaw into the wall, I move my jaws until I feel sharp pain in my worn-down incisors. I taste the blood flowing into my throat.

The crack on the cement surface is only a little bigger.

People are coming. I escape through the window, straight into the sunny, hostile street.

I settled in the sewers. It was safe there. In all the buildings on the street, people were now waging war against rats. Smells irritating the nostrils and the eyes reached sometimes even here, deep underground. I found a lone female, blind in one eye, and I moved into her nest.

You listen to the murmur of flowing sewers, which drowns other sounds. A rat's shrill squeaking pierces this monotonous flow. I get used to it. The whisper of water induces sleep.

But why do you return to the cemented wall of the cellar? Why do you remember it the moment you close your eyes? Why do you wander around near the bakery?

A gray rat with a rounded back and a long hairless tail runs on springy legs across the street, heeding each slight rustle, murmur, movement. Everywhere, at any place, an enemy may skulk. Everywhere, at any hour, death lurks. Life has taught you to fear. You yourself have learned to bite, bite and crush, crush and kill.

All the time, you feel threatened — all the time, from all directions. As the old rat once did, you now visit railway stations, harbors, loading docks, warehouses.

I am at every place from which I can break free, leave the town, wander away. I live in the town, which I hate more and more, which has trapped me, which holds me at bay, the town in which I was born, in which I grew up and became strong.

The one-eyed female is expecting: her enlarged belly and swollen teats exude the smell of approaching motherhood. We bring to the nest anything that can provide warmth. We gather food, which we most often fish out of the dense stream of sewage.

The one-eyed female never leaves the sewer. She is afraid to go above the ground, where she lost her eye. Her life is restricted to a small underground area that she never leaves. The boundaries of her territory are clearly defined: it is encircled by several underground streams, which flow into the broad canal of rainwater. When she reaches it, the one-eyed female stops and retreats. She also retreats from the gray light that falls from above and arouses her suspicion and fear.

The growing urge to wander — violent, obsessive — forces you above the ground. To get out, leave the town, escape. The female gives birth to a litter of rats. The hairless, blind rats squeak, crawl around her belly, raise their heads with difficulty, search for a firmer surface, to stand more securely on their unwieldy legs.

I bring food. The one-eyed female lets me enter the nest, touch the little rats and sniff them.

Autumn rainstorms come. The waters in the sewers are rising. The one-eyed female moves her young to another, much higher, place.

I crossed yards and streets, searching for a fast way out of town.

Even dust and dirt from under the car wheels stimulate, incite you to try again. But traveling by car is dangerous, because you would be close to people, risking a sudden discovery.

You try it once: from the railroad loading dock to the open-air market in another part of town, I ride on a truck filled with fruit. Terrified by the clamor, I flee among the stalls. People almost club me to death with broomsticks. Shaken by the incident, I return to the nest.

The nest is gone; water has flooded the burrow. I follow the tracks of the one-eyed female — first along the wall, later upward. I can hear squeaking. Yet the nest has another, different smell. It smells of another family. The one-eyed female and the little rats haven't yet had time to permeate it with their own scent. Washed by water, their skin is saturated with a sharp, hostile smell. The one-eyed female has already gone through heat and has become indifferent: a strange, unfamiliar rat.

She rubs herself against me, squeezes under my belly. The little rats squeak, move toward me.

With my teeth I grab the closest one and bite him in two. The one-eyed female gets out from under me and covers the young with her body. She holds one of them in her teeth, wanting to carry him to another place. I plunge my teeth into her throat — one, two, three times. She tries to bite me. Weakened, she rolls onto her side, moving her paws chaotically. I kill all the little rats and eat half of each.

I leave the nest. Smelling fresh blood, rats lurk near the wall.

I left the town. I left behind the warm cellars of the bakery, the storerooms full of sweets, the garbage cans with delicious scraps, the labyrinths of sewers and pipes.

I left the cemented nest, the smoothed-out, dead wall, the rats, the people, the lurking traps and poisons.

I left the empty armchair in which only the smell of the young female remained, the trodden rats' paths, the tooth marks on the wooden crates, the trips to the river and the pigpen, the routes I traveled with the old rat. I left the dead one-eyed female and her young that I had ripped to pieces.

I follow the old rat's route, I follow his way. Wind rustles around the train, and the rhythm of the wheels rocks me to sleep. It is cozy, quiet, and warm between the sacks filled with grain. The train is taking me to a faraway city, about which I know nothing. Yet I sense its existence, since that's where the old rat came from and returned to — the old rat whose smell told me about other, distant areas.

Many times I cross the loading dock, where the arms of the cranes lift platforms full of sacks and crates. I search for the scent that will remind me of the old rat. No prior ties link me to the city, and I feel I can leave it. I have to go away because everything in that city that was mine has disappeared, has been obliterated, cemented, destroyed.

I come to know the urge to travel, the necessity to wander.

I hastily cross the streets as if I were fleeing from a dangerous oppressor. I attack other rats, often stronger and bigger than I but settled, placid, sluggish.

I want to part with the city as quickly as possible. Feverish, almost sick, nervous, I often leave the dark tunnels of crevices and sewers to emerge above the ground, among people. They scream, throw rocks at me, beat me with sticks, trample me. I shock them, terrify them, provoke them, and maybe that's why they don't manage to kill me, even though their blows have grazed me.

You hide under a bench in a streetcar. A dog led by a passenger drives you out. The people yell, the dog barks, the streetcar stops. You jump out, straight onto the hood of a slowly moving car. I will always remember the face of the driver who is jerking the steering wheel. The clanging of the metal, the grinding of shattered glass. The car hits a truck that is driving close by. During the commotion I dash through a small window, into a basement room that has a mangle in it. I land on the pile of freshly pressed laundry. Screaming people throw towels at me. I cross under the

59

door to the adjoining cluttered cellar. From there, along the pipes, I get to the sewers.

On the borderline of sleep, listening to the wheels clattering rhythmically on the rails, I recall those incidents. They surround one another, overlap, merge, creating a strange mosaic of memory. I have an illusion that I am in a moving spiral tunnel. I run in it, trying to get outside. But the tunnel has no end, just as it has no beginning, because I have found myself in it unexpectedly, I don't know how. I also move differently. My paws and claws are useless. Inside this immense tunnel I am floating, flying through my own experiences, through the remembered incidents.

I wake up abruptly. A strange rat, a female in heat, strains, exposes her swollen, blood-filled organs, and squeaks. I become aroused. After a moment, we lie down satisfied, next to each other. The female crawls under my head, squeezes under my belly. With my lower jaw I feel her fluffy, warm neck.

The train slows, comes to a halt. We set out to search for water and more varied food. The grain that fills the sacks has a bland taste.

We explore the vicinity. During each such excursion, we have to be careful to come back before the departure of the train. I notice that the rats around me change. Some remain at the railroad stations that we pass, and other rats take their place.

The train stops. A big black rat bursts into our car and at once attacks me with fury.

He chases me around the car for a long time, trying to kill me. Looking for fleas in her thick fur, my new female watches the pursuit indifferently.

The train pulls off. The black rat quits the chase. He

starts feeding on the grain. Hidden at the bottom of the car, inside a sack, I forget about the danger and fall asleep, lulled by the humming noise. I feel a violent pain in my back. With all his weight, the black rat collapses on top of me. I tear his small, hairless ear. Infuriated, he squeaks. We hurl ourselves at each other. He is older, stronger, and seasoned in fights with other rats. Supporting ourselves on our tails, we face each other, spit, squeak, and bare our teeth. His large, exceptionally sharp incisors leave a bloody mark on my back. If he had struck me more toward the middle, between the ears, he would have shattered my spine. We watch each other with hatred, fearing a sudden deadly grip. He springs at my throat and topples me. I turn, I bend, my teeth sink into his fur.

An escape is a chance to survive. I get away to the top of the piles of sacks. I can feel him behind me. I turn and assume an offensive position. Confused by my sudden courage, he stops. I bounce off the tangle of metal ropes that holds the sacks together and leap up into the opening through which air whizzes in.

The wind pushes me back inside. I cling to the rotating paddles. My weight makes them revolve more slowly, and finally they stop. I am outside on the roof of the car.

Convinced that my oppressor will give up further chase, I cling with my belly to the tar-coated surface. Here, in the open space, in the sharp daylight, I feel threatened from all sides. Flattened, I can barely keep my balance. Suddenly the black rat appears. How has he come here? Has he come through the ventilator or found another passage? His teeth cut through the air. I managed to jump aside, and now I'm sliding lower and lower down the rounded roof. The black rat watches me from above. He doesn't attack. I'm no longer dangerous. I'm slipping down. I'm rolling.

The wind tears me off the train and throws me alongside the rumbling tracks.

I run along the railroad tracks, following the sound of the departing train. Night has fallen; a round shiny disk of the moon hangs in the sky. Cold wind blows over me.

Skipping the ties tires me. Small, sharp pebbles badly hurt my paws. I climb to the track — here the path is easy and sufficiently wide. After a while I give up proceeding on top of the track. The bitterly cold metal chills my belly.

I am in a broad, open space. Its vastness is troubling. An encounter with an owl, a cat, a dog is particularly dangerous in such circumstances.

A humming sound that keeps growing louder: a train is coming from the opposite direction. It flies by.

Hidden behind a big white stone, I watch the bright contours of the windows. The train disappears. I keep going. I pass over a bridge, then through a tunnel.

It's getting colder. The moon is covered with a layer of dense, dark clouds.

It's snowing — the first snow in my life. I have to reach a railroad station, get onto a car, continue my journey.

I feed on sausage skins that I have found wrapped in greasy paper. I go ahead. The night will most likely end soon, and then I will have to quit wandering.

Birds fly over the tracks. With all my strength I cling to the wet, snow-covered track. Suddenly I hear a dog panting. He is trailing me. I jump into the ditch. He barks and jumps after me, breaking the thin layer of ice on which I have run safely to the other side. While the angry, yelping dog is clambering up the side of the ditch, I run toward a haystack darkening against the sky.

When I'm near it, I hear the trailing dog bark again. Exhausted, I squeeze into fragrant, dense hay.

I hunt mice that have found shelter from winter in the haystack. A weasel scares me away — a long white creature with narrow and long teeth.

Over the fluffy snow, sinking in it, I go toward nearby buildings. It is snugly warm in the huge barn.

I haven't met any rats so far.

At night I go over to the cowshed. Here I come upon the traces of a female. I find her burrow. There she is, bristling and alarmed at my appearance. She is alone. People have driven away or killed the other rats. Under the floor of the stable, in the pigpen, the henhouse, the house — I go from burrow to burrow. I find rusty traps in the attic. The old poisons indicate a fierce, prolonged war.

You decide to spend the winter in the house lost among the snowdrifts.

At first the female receives me with suspicion. But she soon shows me favor. I find a warm nest located in the foundation of the house. Tunnels lead from it in several directions — to a cellar where barrels of sauerkraut and pickles and jars with various contents stand; to the adjoining henhouse; to the kitchen from which come delicious smells; to the backyard. The last exit is far. It's close to the toolshed.

I am on my guard: I am in a strange, unfamiliar territory. Both the farm buildings and the house are mostly wooden. I gnaw and dig passages to other places. The dog has sensed my presence, and so has the cat. The dog barks when I make my way through the snow toward the house. He also barks when I pass his house. The cat has tracked me down and tried to attack me. I avoid the encounter by escaping to the nearest burrow. Soon we meet eye-to-eye in the corner of the barn, from which it is too late to escape. He attacks me, meowing. I assume a defensive position and stand on my hind paws. The cat stops, surprised at my size and courage. I then spring at him and bite his ears, nose, and neck. Trying to catch my twisting tail, he rakes my back with his claws. He exposes his face. I dig my teeth in his lower jaw. He lets me out of his claws and runs away, terrified.

Bleeding, with a broken paw, a torn back, and a broken tail, I return to the nest. I am sick.

When I am nearby, the cat arches his back, bristles his hair, meows. He is scared. I watch his fear.

I no longer run away. I feel strong, and I often run right in front of him.

A few times, while the people are absent, I chase him away from the stove, where he likes to lie. He hates me. He bares his teeth and snorts.

The people don't notice my presence for a long time. They don't set traps, don't sprinkle poisoned grain, don't scatter deadly substances. The female has her young. In the deeply hidden nest the little rats grow fast. It is warm. Only from the tunnels does cold, harsh air blow.

I bring feathers, down, straw, hay, and even pieces of wood to the nest.

A massive wardrobe standing in one of the rooms mystifies me. When the people leave the house, I immediately gnaw at it. I get inside. Piles of white linens suit my aims perfectly. I bite out a piece of linen and carry it to the nest. I move between the burrow and the wardrobe. I also tear shreds of wool from the clothes hanging in the wardrobe.

Hunting for rats begins once again. The people nail down the hole in the wardrobe, set traps, spread poisoned chicken

64

heads, fish, eggs, cookies, grain. Mice get poisoned in great numbers. After eating smoked fish, the cat dies.

The young rats begin their first unsupervised wanderings.

A few perish, the others survive. By and by they will start building their own nests.

Warmer days come after long-lasting snowstorms and freezing weather, when high snowdrifts surrounded the farmstead.

We, the adult rats, the female and I, don't touch the poisoned delicacies. We recognize them and place our droppings on them.

We have a lot of food in the henhouse, the cowshed, the pigpen, and the pantries.

With my tail I scoop the eggs laid by hens, I eat oats fed to horses, I steal into the pantry, where slabs of bacon, cheeses and sausages, and sacks with flour, groats, and sugar rest.

The snow melts, the winds get warmer, the sun shines.

The next generation of rats leaves the burrow. The females from the first litter are expecting their own young.

Together with a young female you slay all the chickens — tiny, fluffy balls that people let into the henhouse.

The mumbling voices that reach the nest are agitated and violent.

Soon you will leave this house. You will start your trip, your journey to an unknown town that you know exists, full of murky sewers and cellars.

The people stop up the burrows with huge wooden pegs and pour tar on top of them. But for us, rats, digging a new tunnel in the clay or gnawing a hole in rotten boards causes no difficulty. Each nest has several separate exits and tunnels that connect it with nearby burrows.

The urge to wander wakes me up at night. I leave the warm nest, where another litter of tiny rats has arrived.

Across the wet, rain-lashed field, I head for the railroad tracks.

At daybreak you reach the place where the tracks fork and run parallel. Trains pass close by.

The railroad station is nearby.

I quench my thirst in a ditch and look for a suitable train.

While wandering along the tracks I encounter no rats. For the local ones it's still too cold, and they prefer not to leave the warm buildings.

The smell of grain being poured. You approach, squeeze in between humming metal pipes. Rats are pulling and pushing another rat, which lies belly up. A sizable mound of grain lies on his belly, in the hollow between his spread-out paws. The rat adjusts his back so that none of the grain falls. Careful not to hurt him, the others gently clasp his paws and tail and support his sides. They will lug him to the burrow where they stock provisions. The fur on those rats' backs is thinned out from rubbing. They sniff you and issue angry cries. The rat that has been lying on its back throws the grain off and runs toward you.

Your train is standing near a high platform, which will make getting on easy.

A crowd of people terrifies you. You want to escape, to find another way. You stay.

I squeeze in through the waste pipe and hide behind the water tank. Through a half-open door I get into a compartment.

Hidden among the heating installation under a wide seat upholstered with cloth, I watch the movements of human legs. So far I have never been so close to people, I have never listened to their voices from such proximity.

The rocking of the train induces sleepiness. Lying among warm pipes, you are half asleep, half awake, full of memories and associations.

The atmosphere of the warm compartment causes torpor.

You searched for a city. You searched and feared as you always fear the unknown, the uncertain, the new.

The train stops. The passengers get off, new ones get on — they bring in the smell of rain and mud from the streets. We pass unfamiliar places, but they aren't my destination. The old rat was seeking a certain city by its smell, and it's the city I want to reach.

Your nostrils haven't retained that smell, and you will never be sure if you have arrived in the city you sought.

I will recognize that smell at once. I will tell it apart from all others; I will find the town that he wanted to return to. Maybe he escaped from it and later found out that nowhere will he free himself from anxiety, fear, insecurity.

He instilled in you his own rapacity, the urge to wander, and restless dreams. You don't remain long anywhere. You move from place to place, you search.

The people let the window down a little. The compartment is filled with a cold, moist breeze — a sign that a great body of water is nearby. I wake up. I breathe air into my nostrils. You are coming to your destination.

The rhythmic clatter of the tracks ends. The train passes switch after switch. The people collect their packages, close their bags and suitcases.

The station. The train has stopped. The people are leaving the compartment. The last of them slams the sliding door.

I wait until the noise in the corridor subsides. I am locked in. I jump on the seat and the windowsill. Not even the smallest chink. I toss around in the compartment. With fury I scratch and bite the door.

You have come to a town. You can recognize its indistinct contours from the window, but you can't leave the locked box.

The rat runs in the narrow space, climbs the shelves. He doesn't notice that the train has pulled out and is going farther.

It stops on a side track. You bang your head on the windows and walls, you gnaw in many different places, trying to get out.

Early in the morning, when the first gray light has come in through the window, a cleaning woman opens the door. You leap out, brushing against her feet.

She screams, hits the floor with a rag attached to a pole.

The door of the car is open. You jump into the fog that hangs over the tracks.

Toward evening, on a torrid day, when you were running across the yard in the back of a restaurant, a rock flew right by your head. It bounced off the brick wall of the garbage container and slowed down. It landed in a pile of tin cans, reverberating loudly in the dark shaft of the yard. The echoes pursued you a little longer, bouncing off the smooth walls and glass surfaces in the cellar full of demijohns bubbling with wine.

You always pass the cool cellar, and through a long tunnel you come to the air shaft that connects with the kitchen. It is very hot here, and warm wafting air brings aromas that stimulate your hunger and entice you.

You climb a steep, unplastered wall and enter the adjoining pipe. Walking in almost complete darkness, you let your whiskers, your sense of smell, and the texture of the ground guide you. Your paws sink into a thin layer of ashes: you are in a boiler room, from which warm water reaches all segments of the house.

It's close. Most houses have several levels of cellars — and for a long time people haven't visited the ones that are sealed, forgotten, that lie deep underground. The cellars belong only to us — to rats. We feel safe in them, we aren't hunted and chased, there are no traps or poisons. Even cats avoid the underground, afraid that we would outnumber them.

My nest is located on the lowest level in a huge brick cellar, among furniture crumbling from age. There are many rats' nests here on the floor or inside decayed wardrobes and cupboards. I am the strongest, the largest, the fastest among the rats that inhabit nearby cellars.

The local rats have accepted me, have let me settle in this unknown sea town.

From the cellar, reinforced with strong wooden ties, you can get to neighboring underground passages, to dungeons that run under all of the old section of town, to sewers, and to the port. Most of the passages have been built by people. Many furrows have been eroded by water and by the sliding soil. The rats have connected them by a net of their own tunnels and corridors.

Here in the deep cellars, even the seasons don't disturb the rhythm of our life. Only water that floods some of the cellars during violent rainstorms puts us in danger.

My females get along well. They take turns watching their young, procuring food, guarding the safety of the nests. Occasionally they confuse their young, and that causes shoving and minor biting.

When you found yourself on the vast expanse of tracks in

the dense white fog, terrified by bitter cold, you wanted to slip back into the car again. That lasted a moment. The distant sound of the ship's siren resounding over the old town called you in that direction.

Suspicious, scared, bristled up, you walked in the fog across the tracks toward the unknown sound.

I trudged across the tracks, I roamed huge junkyards, I squeezed through a high wire fence. I ran across the street right in front of an enormous car, through an overpass above the tracks, through the wide strip of the park. The sound of the siren pointed the direction.

I found myself in the tangle of streets in the old section of town, among narrow houses. Immediately you smelled many rats' nests. That terrified you, even though it was quiet and tranquil all around. Through a half-open window you got to the nearest cellar, and there you encountered the first of the local rats, who carefully sniffed your drenched fur.

You ran away from him. He ran after you through cellars and corridors.

You lost him. You were by yourself; now you could sleep and rest. You woke up: rats had gathered around you. They touched you with their whiskers, they sniffed you, they grazed you with their teeth.

Fear overpowered and paralyzed me. I was in the middle, among them, I was afraid to stir. The situation was upsetting. The rats watched my behavior, tested my endurance. I tried to act as if nothing threatened me. With my nose I touched the nearest one, showing my strong teeth at the same time.

He retreated. I rested on my hind paws and began grooming. I washed for a long time, I licked dust off my fur, I smoothed single hairs, I picked fleas.

70

The rats awaited my reaction. They would have attacked me long before if it hadn't been for my composure, my size, my teeth.

I was afraid, I was upset, and with each moment I had a hard time preserving my imperturbable attitude.

But they didn't do anything to you. You fell asleep in a rats' nest, and your wet fur helped you absorb a new odor. You began to smell like local rats. The females tensed at the sight of you. I saw, but I wasn't aware of that. I felt I was an alien rat. I was scared.

A shrill cry of a cat lured by our presence. He meows at the door, claws and bites the old boards.

We escape to another cellar.

I get to know the city. I wander. It's different from the one I left. It's inhabited by vicious rats. I am chased away a few times. The pursuit is short — rats avoid open battles.

An abundance of food is within easy reach, garbage cans full of scraps every day. Easily accessible store and cafeteria pantries, markets, warehouses with exotic fruit, elevators full of wheat and other grains. Rats fill their stomachs unhindered.

A great city, the city of feasting, the city of satiety.

That's how you remember it, that's how it was the first few days after your arrival.

At present you feel alarmed because even here, in the cellars that are deep underground, there's a nervous atmosphere, fear, and foreboding.

The sounds of explosions, the detonations, the shaking of the earth, the vibrations of the walls, at first reach me from far away, from a long distance, but they are approaching. I can hear them clearly.

71

I don't know what they mean and to what extent they can endanger me. Falling asleep, I listen carefully to those strange sounds that come from the depth of the earth, and I try to guess their meaning, to figure out their cause.

The distant echoes no longer approach. They have stopped in one place; they don't move. They resemble thunder that follows lightning and rolls over the city.

Yet those echoes aren't thunder. They are different: heavy, crushing. They shake the earth, the buildings, the foundations.

The foreboding of a disaster causes violent reactions in rats. They suffer from insomnia, they ignore danger, on the spur of the moment they attack stronger animals, they often move to another place, they behave contrary to their normal behavior.

Your anxiety has increased because of the behavior of the people who are leaving the city, departing in panic. Many apartments stand empty. You take advantage of that, you venture into unfamiliar places full of bright light and air. You get to know furniture and human implements — beds, couches, tables, bookcases, wardrobes, cupboards, chairs, curtains, lamps. You visit rooms, kitchens, bathrooms. You discover that you can get to every room through a chimney flue. If the flue has a grating, then you can go through the water-filled opening in the toilet bowl, a device until now unfamiliar to you. It's enough to pass through a thin layer of water and go down a wide pipe to the nearest sewer.

This simplest connection of human dwellings with the underground world has saved your life many times.

The sounds become more powerful; they come from the outskirts of the city.

Then, right then, you found out how fragile and weak your greatest enemy — the human — really is.

He appears inside an underground passage. In his hand he holds a flashlight that throws exceptionally bright light. He moves quickly onward, his stooping figure blocking the narrow corridor through which many rats make their daily trips. On his head he wears a helmet, which reflects the light beams. Alarmed and irritated, rats run past him, slip between his legs, brush against his helmet and shoulders.

The man is walking faster and faster. Suddenly the loud squeak of a rat that has been crushed is heard. The passage leads to the lowest, long-forgotten cellar. People have bricked up its exit. Only the stairs, ending with a blind brick wall, have remained. We rats have many exits out of here, but they are inaccessible to a human.

The cellar swarms with rats. The sudden entry of a human causes confusion. He stands still, shines the light on the cellar, notices the contour of the stairs, and starts in their direction.

We hurl ourselves at him. We attack him. He runs to the stairs, shines his light on the wall, and, seeing the bricked rectangle, decides to escape the way he has come. He shakes some rats off himself. As hard as he can, he flings one against the wall and shatters the spine of another.

He blinds us with the light. He is approaching the door when he suddenly stumbles and crushes a little rat, still blind. A furious female leaps straight at his face. He drops the flashlight. Its beams now shine vertically, drawing a circle of light on the ceiling.

I attack him, I bite, cut the fabric, the skin, the flesh.

He fights, kills, crushes. With all my strength I bite his neck, I push myself under the metal helmet. Other rats do the same. The helmet falls down.

The man kneels, gropes for the flashlight, but can no longer reach it.

Blood floods his eyes, his face, his hands. He is kneeling, overrun by a gray mass of rats.

He screams, howls, mumbles.

A rat thrusts itself into his mouth. The man cuts him with his teeth, spits, moans, grows silent.

He rolls over. Rats come running from all directions.

The nervousness increases. The less hardened rats leave the old section of the city. They move, but there are no peaceful places. The noise that is steadily growing louder can be heard all over the city. Now and then it subsides, dies, only to return again — still louder and more terrifying. During rare moments of quiet, the rats recover their composure. They delude themselves that everything has gone back to the previous state.

There is a shortage of food, there is a shortage of everything that the rats living in that city got used to: fish, meat, grain, food, refuse.

Most pantries are empty. Aromatic slabs of bacon, sacks of groats, peas, beans, piles of fruit, have disappeared from the huge market. Even the elevators, which until now have been full of wheat, oats, and other grains, are empty.

Those changes have happened fast, no one knows when. In the wide-open apartments, kitchens and pantries are also empty. Leaving behind the furniture and household effects, people have taken all the food with them.

The rats have long ago eaten everything edible in the garbage cans.

Conflicts, quarrels, fights, erupt. A defeated, knocked-down rat is immediately devoured. Strangers aren't tolerated now. On the contrary, they are hunted, tracked, killed.

Incidents in which mothers devour their young also take place more and more frequently.

One night the thundering noise moves directly into the vicinity of the old town: it slips in, crawls toward it, fills it.

The wind drives clouds of acrid smoke. The rats hide in the deepest cellars and burrows.

Fire: the old town is burning. The houses collapse, the walls tremble, the ceilings crack.

Smoke and the smell of burning reach deep underground.

You leave the dangerous cellars with a crowd of rats.

Rats are coming out from all the gates, corridors, cellars, dungeons — stunned, terrified, distracted, half alive, feverish.

The wind blows over the burning roofs. It sprinkles everything with sparks. Frantic rats rush headlong, their numbers growing every moment, to get farther away from the fire and the smoke. Burned, injured, blinded, they are escaping the blazing city.

I am in the first line that has reached the moat encircling the old town. The ditch now is filled up with rats swimming to the other bank. Many drown, many others run over the backs and heads of those that are swimming. The opposite side is near. I jump onto the sloping bank.

Here also the houses are on fire. The explosions shower us with burning particles, fragments of plaster and bricks, dust.

People escape at the sight of us. Terrified, they flee and hide in the hallways of the buildings that are about to collapse.

We join other groups of rats. There are more and more of us, and even though a lot of us perish, our numbers are increasing. At one point I jump onto a barrel.

Around me I see a vast sea of rats' backs, filling the street as far as the horizon. We are walking now along the port canals toward the still-peaceful sea.

All night, all night long, exhausted, surrounded by smoke, dust, stench, the odor of burning, slashing rain, we jump over water-filled ditches, cross swamps, sandy dunes, gardens, orchards.

We reach distant districts of the city, we scatter in the street in search of hiding places. The wind, permeated with the odor of burning, suddenly changes direction. I can smell the nearby sea.

The winds blow almost incessantly. They induce runny noses, headaches, insomnia. After the long stay in the old district, living close to the sea seems hard at first. You slowly get used to the new climate. You get to know the salty, brisk smell of the sea, the murmur of the rolling waves, the proximity of the unfamiliar element.

I live in a low brick building. It has a sloping roof covered with tiles that are often knocked off by the wind. It has cellars that are shallowly sunken into the ground.

In the room under the porch I discover a faucet identical to the one from my native town. Maybe that's why I build my nest here under the stairs. I can hear each step the people make, but I quickly become accustomed to those sounds, and soon they stop making an impression on me. Naturally, my hiding place has several extra exits. It is connected to the neighboring cellar, as well as to the ends of the chimney flues. That allows me to wander into all apartments in the building. But the most interesting passage is the one that leads under the floor of the nearest apartment, located on the first floor. Unhindered and safe, I can listen there to the sounds uttered by people and breathe pleasant kitchen smells. Before long I also discover passages under the floors of apartments in the neighboring houses. Through air shafts I easily make my way to the second floor and to the attic that has been converted into an apartment.

The brick house stands on a quiet, not too busy street. Many fruit trees and bushes grow behind the backyard. This small orchard is surrounded by sheds, hovels, booths, pigpens, henhouses, small gardens, crates, cages with rabbits, and pigeon coops that lean against the neighboring houses.

The rats that came here with you wandered farther on since, when it rains, the sewers in this district fill up with water and become uninhabitable. Many rats drowned. Others wandered along the seashore, looking for more hospitable quarters. Some of them settled in the cellars or under the floors of local houses, in the port buildings, warehouses, grain elevators, under overpasses, on the sides of ditches, dams, and irrigation canals.

I quickly realized that the major canal flows across the district, connecting the sea with the town, with docks, ports, warehouses.

Passing ships signal their arrival with prolonged hooting of the siren. Already back then you were pondering another trip. Your new house is very close to the route of the passing ships. You often venture inside the port, you stroll on the stone embankment, you look down at the oil-covered water, which reflects the moon.

It is enough to cross the yard, the parallel street, and the row of buildings behind it, then several pairs of tracks, to get to the vast embankments stretching along the canal. Sometimes you go down the rough steps to the level of sluggish waves and walk on huge logs covered with seaweeds and shells. You find there tiny fish, small crabs, clams, snails. They add variety to your fairly monotonous food stolen from hens and pigs.

It gets warmer, and you decide to return to the old part of town. You begin to miss the long underground corridors, the sewers, the cellars.

You go back. The town is in ruins. A large number of the sewers and underground cellars have collapsed, caved in. The smell of burning permeates everything. The disagreeable stench of smoke is disappearing very slowly. The first rats, which devour carrion, have already settled in the rubble.

In the ruins, in the cellars that any moment can be buried under layers of rubble, I discover decomposing human corpses, dead dogs, cats, rats. Predatory birds ceaselessly hover over the destroyed town.

I return to the brick house in the port district, where I can smell the sea and where constantly blowing winds play unusual whistling tunes in the ventilating shafts.

You lead the life of a typical rat who plunders metal garbage cans, digs new passages and tunnels, steals delicacies hidden in warehouses and pantries.

A journey full of dangers, trials, struggles, and quests awaits you. You will wander farther and farther, only to want to return even more.

You remember: in the night you went close to the ships, you looked at thick mooring ropes, at anchor cables, the open trapdoors, cranes. You went there, even though hungry dogs and dangerous cats roamed the port, and owls hovered noiselessly over the dimly lit wharves. Why did you risk your life to the teeth, beaks, claws?

Ships arouse my interest. I see in them floating fragments of land on which — as on a train — you can travel over vast areas with relatively little effort.

In your native town, in the company of the old rat, you often ventured out to the river port, which was full of barges. The old rat, daunted by a distant unpleasant incident, rarely came on their decks. He was also scared of big seagulls flying over the water.

You noticed that the rats inhabiting the barges jealously guarded their narrow territory and attacked more viciously than the rats in other sections of your town.

I end my wanderings in front of a ship. I come close to it — as close as possible. Standing on my hind paws, I touch the strong ropes with my whiskers and withdraw. I return to my safe burrow, to my labyrinth, its corridors and passages running through the long brick house and the adjacent buildings.

You are afraid to enter the ship, you are afraid to break away from the hard, stony wharf.

I don't want to leave, I am used to the surroundings, the house, the garbage cans, the trodden paths, the human voices. I already know each corner, each bend in the wall, the grooves in the plaster, the chinks, the cobwebs, the stains on the wall.

You are getting ready for the journey. You are waiting for the events that will allow you to sail away and leave that city behind you.

A gray shadow flits through the gutters of the port streets. At the slightest sound, it clings to the ground, blends into the flagstones. Suddenly it stops and listens to the tones of the flute coming from the window.

You go there all the time. The sounds that attract you are coming from the house on the same street. From a distance you hear them the moment the man begins to play. At once you leave the nest. Other rats are heading there too. The man doesn't even know how many rats are listening to him. They come from every side. They climb the rainwater pipe, clamber onto the roof, squeeze into the chimney flues and vents, go up the trees, slink on the balcony railing, hug the walls.

The sounds that the man forces out of a dark, elongated pipe daze, call, summon. You want to be as near their source as possible, to reach the place where they originate, to get to know their cause, to touch it.

The man is playing. His bent silhouette stands out clearly against the lit-up curtain. Every day when the sun sinks below the horizon and birds get ready to sleep, he plays, even though from the apartments below come different sounds — mumbling and yelling, which drown the tones of his instrument. The moment he starts playing, the people who live below behave unusually noisily.

I'm running. I'm coming closer and closer to the source of the sounds. All around, rats are coming out of every cellar and nook. The deserted street is full of oblong moving shadows. Under the balcony from which the music comes, the plants stir as if touched by the wind.

You try to get there as close as possible. Taking advantage of the vines that grow on the walls of the house, you climb to the balcony and slip inside. From the level of a bookshelf, you watch the man holding to his lips a long black pipe, from which issue the tones that transform you, alter you, vanquish you. Petrified, motionless, stunned, I listen to the music as if it were a dream, although it isn't a dream.

The man quits playing. He takes the instrument from his lips, dismantles it, and puts it into an oblong case, which he closes. I recover my mobility. The surrounding world again terrifies me. I'm scared; every rustle threatens me.

The music calms me, gives me a sense of complete security. It lets me forget about the necessity of procuring food, gnawing, searching for new passageways, about constant vigilance, about the fear of being attacked by a cat, an owl, a fox, or strange rats. This music frees me of fear, soothes me, puts me in a state of wonderful stupefaction.

You want to follow the music everywhere, wherever it will lead you. Since the moment you heard it for the first time, you have felt the need to listen to it always. You wait for it every evening, and on the days when the old man doesn't pick up the instrument, you feel sick, upset, restless. Other rats behave more aggressively than usual. They assail each other, bite, run around nervously, and even attack people.

The man doesn't notice the rats. He doesn't see them gather around the house and listen to his music.

The street he lives on leads to the port, straight to the wharf where ships moor. I remember the loud cry of a man bitten by a rat on whose tail he has stepped in the darkness.

The old man immediately stops playing and comes on the balcony. The rats, listening raptly till then, scamper in every direction. Hidden in the scraps of paper lying next to the wall, you listen to the unintelligible sounds uttered by the people who have gathered in the street.

The next day, at the usual time, before taking the instrument out of the case, the man opens the balcony door and places his chair in such a way that he can see clearly what goes on in the bright circle of light from the gas lamp.

When he starts playing, the rats as usual begin to head toward the house, stopping for a moment right at the border of the light and then hastily hopping into the lit area.

There are more and more of them. He watches them — the gray shadows dazed, motionless, listening raptly.

Since then he has always played, carefully watching our behavior.

Meanwhile the tenants from the first floor and from the neighboring houses try all possible means to drown out his music. They turn on various appliances, they make noise, they shriek.

Evening. I have just climbed the gutter and hidden myself on the shelf. I can see clearly each movement of the fingers on the elongated shape that the man is holding to his lips.

Suddenly he stops playing. Heavy steps can be heard on the staircase. The door opens with a crash. Terrified, I cling to the shelf.

The people burst in. They scream. They snatch the instrument, break it, trample over it. He tries to wrest it back. They struggle. The man is lying on the floor. They beat him, kick him.

They leave as abruptly as they came in. The thudding noise made by their feet can still be heard on the stairs. The bloodied man is lying curled up on the floor. I quickly jump off the shelf, slink onto the balcony, and slide down the gutter.

He tries to restore his instrument. He fits the broken pieces as if believing that they will grow back together. He presses the protruding splinters with his fingers. He spreads glue on the pieces, ties them with thin wires. It doesn't work. When he tries playing, the flute breaks into pieces and crumbles. The man lays it on the table and returns to bed. He is lying still.

I come back. The man moans, groans, wakes up screaming. His face is swollen, cut, with black patches where he was struck.

The days go by. The man gets up, leaves the house, comes back. Again he lies down, facing the wall. His back moves spasmodically.

When I slip into the apartment again, he lies motionless on the bed. Next to him, on the table, candles are burning.

Go near. Along the baseboard. Go under the bed. Try to reach the folded hands of the man by climbing the blanket that is hanging down — as dull as your fur. Sniff his hands carefully, touch them with your whiskers. They are cold, still, lifeless. The man is dead. The sudden scream of a person sitting nearby and the violent movements toward you scare you away.

I escape through the open door to the balcony, among the tall flowers growing in the garden.

Throughout the rest of my stay in the port, until the beginning of the journey, I deeply miss the music — I miss the sounds that the man used to play.

This feeling is as strong as hunger or thirst, and it can't be stifled in any way — quite as if I had been suddenly deprived of a vital organ or body part.

Other rats who, like me, used to come here are now irritated, bristling, restless. They linger in the neighboring sewers and cellars as if waiting for the moment when they will suddenly hear the soothing, luring sounds.

You also wait for the sound that will suddenly reach the sewer, make you forget your rat's wanderings, and force you to listen. You wait, even though a while ago you touched his lifeless hands with your whiskers and smelled the familiar odor of death. Still you wait, you run, you circle.

I search for another man with the same instrument. I find

him several streets away. I find him, but the sounds that issue from the instrument that looks the same don't make me restless, don't make me wander toward them at once, don't move or overpower me. On the contrary, their jarring tones vibrate in my ears, increasing my nervousness. The strange sounds clash with the memories of those other sounds, which my rat's brain has retained, that other music, which keeps coming back.

Sharp, cold winds that reach almost everywhere are blowing in the port. Icy rainstorms begin. They flood the cellars and transform the sewers into streams of rushing water.

You decide to leave the city. Large ships moored along the wharf lure you.

The sudden absence of the flute music has upset my whole nervous system, weakened my vigilance, blunted my distrust of new and unfamiliar things. Agitated, I scurry through the sewers and the cellars, listening to the sounds that come from above. I want to make sure that they don't resemble the marvelous tones of the destroyed instrument. When I happen to hear sounds that are only somewhat similar, I immediately go above the ground in search of their source.

Before long I realize that my wanderings under the city — below the normal level of human life — severely restrict my chances of finding a man playing the flute. The sounds from the apartments on upper floors — and there are many such apartments in the city — barely reach the cellars. The solid foundations of tall buildings effectively muffle all the sounds coming from them. So I decide to search for the music above the ground, almost among people.

I wander inside garbage chutes, old chimneys, vents and chinks. I also often squeeze into sewer pipes and cross streams of water. I climb the rough walls of houses or walk from one roof to another. Naturally, those expeditions are risky. The claws of owls and cats are ready to strike.

It was then that the incident incompatible with everything you knew disturbed you.

My house, the red-brick house. I run to the cellar and through the chink in the door get inside. I am hungry. It's bright in the cellar. The light comes in through the glass at the top of the door.

The sunbeams reach deep inside. They brighten the clean, whitewashed walls and the heavy wooden door. It's cozy and quiet. The smell of fresh smoked bacon fills the cellar. I discover the source of the smell at once: a big slab glistening with fat lies inside an oblong metal box that opens on one side.

I walk around it, I sniff it carefully. The cage is made of thin steel bars. Their ends are driven into a thick board. I find the marks of rats' teeth on it. The rats must have been sharpening their incisors on its surface. I come near the open door. The bacon looks especially appetizing from this side. It's fat, aromatic, tender — it's been long since I ate something like that. More and more saliva collects in my mouth.

A few movements, and the delicious morsel will end up between my teeth. I feel gnawing, painful hunger. My stomach contracts and expands, and my jaws move rhythmically, as if they were already crushing the tasty skin.

I forget about caution, I forget about danger, I forget about human ruses. If it's a trap, maybe I'll be able to snatch the food and flee. The hunger pushes me inside. I can't resist this force. Slowly I enter the cage. First I cautiously stick my head in, then I place my front paws on the wooden bottom, watching out for danger. I calm down.

I am already inside, only the tip of my tail sticking out of the cage. The smell of the smoked bacon absorbs me completely. I sniff it — a big piece that will surely be enough for a meal.

I lick it. It has the delicate salty taste of fried fat and meat.

I have to grab it quickly with my teeth and carry it out of the cage, which still worries me. I plunge my incisors into the dark layer of meat. A sudden crash. It's the door in the back that has fallen. The piece of bacon is attached to a lever that is connected to the door by a spring. If I had stood on my hind paws and looked at the top of the cage, I would have discovered the device, which I have seen in many traps. The intoxicating smell of the bacon deprived me entirely of caution.

I storm around the cage. I try to bite the metal bars until my gums are bleeding. In vain. I gnaw the oak wood. The marks indicate that many rats have been here before me. But I keep gnawing in hope that I'll manage to free myself.

Judging by the smell of the still-warm bacon, the trap has been placed here only recently. Gnawing a hole in such a sturdy board would take long.

People will surely come before I could do it. I carefully inspect the interior of the cage, seeking at least the shadow of a chance of freeing myself. For some time I try to push out the door, to lift it, to pry it open.

Now I notice strong steel springs that support the door on the other side. When I was circling the trap, I didn't see them. They were raised together with the tin trapdoor.

I squirm, jump, fling myself around.

Finally, resigned, I sit and start eating the bacon. This action engrosses me completely. I eat the very last bit.

The sun has set; it's dark. The light from a bulb burning above the door falls in through the window.

I hurl myself at the bars, I gnaw the steel until my gums hurt, I strike the metal door with my head, I squeeze my nostrils between the bars. I jump, trying to overturn the cage with my weight. Everything fails. Tomorrow people will come, drag me out, and kill me. Before that they may blind me or break my spine. Maybe they'll throw me into a metal barrel standing in the yard and from above toss burning paper, stones, pieces of glass. Maybe they'll drop me into a sack and strike the wall with it as hard as they can. I know what people do with rats. I saw many times how people killed them. They may not come here for a few days, until I die from exhaustion, anxiety, and thirst. I can't escape, I won't gnaw through the hard, thick bottom. I won't have enough strength.

In the dark I hear voices coming from upstairs, the voices of the people who have set the trap. A gray shadow flits by, approaches cautiously, touches the cage with whiskers. It's a local rat, for whom the trap was probably intended. After a while another one appears. They circle, watch. They try the steel springs with their teeth. They leave.

A large cat comes from inside the cellar. He has sensed my presence and is ready to spring. He's already close to me. Meowing shrilly, he tries to squeeze his paw between the bars. He can't do anything to me. The bars resist. I feel his breath. Round shining eyes look at me from above.

He rests his paw on the cage. I bite the black, soft pad. He cries, spits, jerks the joints of the bars. In vain. For a little while he circles the trap, meowing. At last, lured by rustling from the other end of the cellar, he retreats.

I want to drink, I want to drink more and more. The salty bacon eaten to the last bit demands water. My throat burns. I feel queasy. I'm about to choke. I start gnawing a hole in the hard board again. I gnaw until I feel that my incisors have been ground down. The rats come back; they circle the cage. They bite my tail, which sticks inadvertently through the bars.

They escape. The cat comes again. I rest motionless in the middle of the cage and watch him walk around it.

I close my eyes: memories appear. The old rat fighting with a cat. Father driving me out of the nest. The death of the little female scalded by boiling water. A multitude of images hidden deeply, retained forever. The man playing the flute. The people are beating him. They bend over the cage, crush me with their boots. I squeak sharply.

It's morning already. I feel burning thirst. I try to groom myself, to catch in my fur at least a few fleas full of blood. But the fleas are unusually active and restless. They sense my fever and a new odor in my sweat.

The cage is low. I can't sit on my tail and hind paws. I bite the wood again. People are already waking up above me. I press furiously on the metal hatch. I storm, jump, push, tense my muscles. I am more and more exhausted, more and more terrified.

Death is approaching: if people don't come and kill me, the situation I'm in will destroy me — the sudden loss of freedom, my imprisonment in a steel cage, lack of water.

I hear mumbling voices, the sounds of food being cooked, a barking dog, creaking boards, running water, movement. I give up. I sit still, with the tip of my tail tucked under my jaw. I wait.

Fast, hurried steps on the stairs. A human is approaching. He'll kill me right away.

Again I struggle in the cage, looking for an opportunity — maybe I'll slip away when he's taking me out of the cage.

The door opens, it creaks loudly.

The man stands over the cage. He bends. I notice the eyes,

the mouth, the skin on the face, moving with every breath. He makes mumbling, squeaking sounds.

We look at each other for a long while. My tail is again out of the cage. He touches it, squeezes it lightly with his fingers. I turn around abruptly, I cling to the opposite wall. I shiver with fear. He'll kill me, he will surely kill me.

The man opens his mouth again. I hear squeaky mumbling that is clearly intended for me. I cower, press into the corner.

With his hand he presses the lever that protrudes over the cage. The springs creak. The hatch rises.

The man attaches the lever to the metal shank. The cage is open. He doesn't do anything. He kicks the cage, encouraging me to exit.

In a flash I leap out, run past his motionless feet. Through a chink in the cellar door, I get outside and hide in a garbage can. From there I move to a pigpen that leans against a wooden shed.

I quench my thirst.

My past knowledge of people, everything I knew about them, contradicts this incident.

He didn't kill me but let me out. Maybe I outsmarted him. Maybe I seemed weak, incapable of escaping. Maybe he concluded that I was dead. But he encouraged me to leave the cage. He moved it, kicked it with his foot. Maybe I imagined it, maybe I hallucinated, dreamed. I know I didn't.

A waft of moist autumn air chills me. Scared, on stiff, straight legs so as not to muddy my belly, I run toward the port.

I set out. At night, hidden in a pile of sacks filled with sugar, I get on a ship. I remember the rocking of the crane and the grating of the chains that lifted the heavy platform.

The entire hold is filled with sacks of sugar, and the hold next to it is piled with sacks of grain.

Walking from one compartment to another, I am surprised near the kitchen by a huge cat. He steals up on me while I am grooming myself, and I suddenly see his wide-open, shining eyes behind me.

I immediately scream to scare him away. I assume a defensive posture: I huddle up as if ready to spring, supporting my whole body on my hind paws and my tail.

The cat looks at my bristled hair and then calmly sits across from me. He moistens his paw with spittle and begins to wash.

I take advantage of that and run away. Later I find out that the cat has never hunted rats, never fought us. Well-fed and fat, he lies still in the middle of the deck on sunny days, paying no attention to what goes on around him. I see seagulls land on his back — they must have assumed he was an inanimate object. He then gets up, stretches, and again lies down to sleep.

Accustomed to his presence, the ship's rats circle him, approach him, sniff his head, paws, tail. He never attacks, bites, or claws a rat. I have seen that, but I can't believe it. Throughout my whole stay on the ship I have suspected a ruse and tried to keep away from the cat.

The first encounter with the sea takes place at night. So far you have known only small waves striking the hull. Now the rocking has become more intense, and the crash of water on the sheathing of the hull has become more severe.

Soon the engine roars, the ship shakes, quivers. Here, in the hold, you feel those vibrations with exceptional intensity. You become nervous, you can't get used to them, and for a long time you suffer from sleeplessness.

90

The hatches are down, and it's almost completely dark in the holds.

I am in a place that can't be left.

I familiarized myself with the confined area of the ship before it sailed. But back then I could abandon it at any minute, even by jumping in the water and swimming to the shore.

You have ended up in a closed space surrounded by hostile, rough elements, not knowing where you're going.

The incessant rocking, which takes away my appetite and induces vomiting, bothers me most. Now and then the rocking becomes so forceful that it causes the crates and the sacks in the holds to move. You escape being crushed between loose crates, which crash at the place where you were sleeping a moment ago. Warned by the moaning of wood rubbing against the floor, you jump away at the last moment. The crates pinch the tip of your tail, which becomes blue and swollen.

Setting out for your journey, you didn't anticipate such a long stay in an iron box. You didn't know what waiting and impatience meant. Now you run frantically inside, scared and angry, dreaming of going ashore, to the normal, quiet, solid ground, which doesn't rock or vibrate.

It's calmer; the rocking becomes bearable. Again a sudden change in the weather. The ship tilts, the steel walls creak under the impact of the mass of water. It creates the impression that the ship is about to break to pieces. The air in the holds gets stuffy, charged with electricity. My fur rises, causing my skin to itch unpleasantly. My whiskers, touching the crates and the ground, discharge tiny sparks. Loose crates and loads move in every direction, turn over, roll.

Terrified and stupefied, most rats hide in inaccessible

nooks, inside pipes and shafts, next to the ribs and the keel, near walls, among heavy and immobile loads. The hard surface under their paws gives them a temporary sense of security, makes them believe they will endure.

The rumbling, banging, crashing noises, the howling wind everywhere, the hollow lashing of the waves. The rats are unable to endure the strain. They leave their hideouts in search of more peaceful, more tranquil places. But there are none. The force of inertia throws them among the sliding crates.

On spread-out paws, like lifeless objects, they crawl on the bottom of the hold. With difficulty they reach seemingly safer places among the sacks filled with sugar. Suddenly a rope snaps, and the sacks tumble, straight down on a rat that is moving below. They grind him into pulp.

The storm continues. I am tired, more and more tired. I fall into a state of drowsiness. I'm awakened by very strong jolts. The awareness that there's nowhere to escape, that in all the areas of the ship it is the same — this awareness immobilizes me, pushes me against the hard casing of the air pipes. I have to wait for the storm to pass.

You wake up. The storm still continues, but the effects of the rocking aren't so painful anymore. Your organism adjusts quickly. You recover a sense of balance, and you aren't terrified when the ship tilts or jolts. You're used to hearing the roaring waves, the clattering and groaning of metal. Moving among the sacks, crates, and barrels that tumble down and slide seems easier, almost natural, as if you had stayed among threatening, animate objects since the first days of your life. The storm is over. People tie broken ropes, remove torn sacks, shore up the crates.

I get used to shaking and rocking. I stop noticing them, recognizing as natural what terrified me a while ago. Even the vibrations of the screw propeller and the roaring of the ventilators — the sound of the air forced into the pipes — make no impression on me.

All the time you wait for the moment when the ship will touch land. Maybe that's why in the night you go out so often on the deck, among the coils of rope and anchor chains. You listen to the murmuring of the sea and the rustling of the wind.

It will happen soon; you anticipate that moment. You'll climb down the mooring cable or run down the accommodation ladder to the shore, and you will begin another journey forward. In search, in search of food. But here, on the ship, there's a lot of food. Nor did you lack food in the deserted cities. There was often more food than you could eat, than all the rats could eat. I run restlessly on the cold floor of the hold. I feel a growing urge to wander.

The ship is moored near a port. At night I go out on the deck, and from a coil of ropes I notice the lights. The wind blowing from land carries unsettling smells — of fire, ashes, smoke, dust. I'm familiar with these odors, I remember them well.

Now I feel anxious. The sounds of explosions and shooting come from the foreign city. Only the closest buildings seem safe, still, dark, dead.

The proximity of the port uncommonly excites all the rats that inhabit the ship. But the ship is no longer moving; it is resting in one spot, not far away from the shore. The engines have stopped working, the rocking has stopped.

After a long rest the ship comes to the shore. The sound of wooden logs being crushed between the high stone wharf and the ship's side reverberates in all the holds. It's night.

I go out onto the dark deck. Under the lifeboats I run toward the exit. The accommodation ladder is only half-way down.

Disregarding the danger, I jump.

The situation in the city has become unbearable. Missiles explode, houses burn, smoke fills the cellars. The odor of burning kills other smells.

Clouds of smoke and fog, of soot and scorched paper, hang over the port, which is surrounded by burning districts.

My foray to warehouses and the closest buildings almost ends in tragedy. A missile exploding nearby deprives me for some time of hearing. Half alive, I'm lying on my side, in an unnatural position. The explosion has hurled me against the window of what used to be a store. A man appears, grabs me by the tail. I turn back and abruptly bite his finger.

The man — I can see it in his eyes and in the motions of his gaunt jaws — is hungry, and he has decided to eat me. I'm his chance, his chance for survival. Staggering, he runs after me along the street, but he can't overtake me.

I want to return to the ship; it's my only goal. So far I haven't run into rats. There are no cats and dogs. They have been eaten by starving, wounded people.

Fear seizes me: if the ship leaves, I'll be lost. I will stay forever in this terrifying city, among explosions, empty port warehouses, ravenous people hunting for rats.

Wind, contaminated by the odor of smoke, is blowing from the port. I proceed in that direction. The smell of smoke and of corpses decomposing under the rubble lingers in my nostrils.

I see people in the open space, next to the wall. They

stand facing one another: one group in the full sun, with their hands tied and black bands across their eyes; the other in the middle of the square, with raised rifles. Bang. People are killing people. They go away, leaving the corpses in the dust, surrounded by the buzzing of large blue flies.

I'm thirsty. I cautiously approach the stream of flowing blood. From the opposite end, from the opening under the wall, an old rat emerges. The rat has a dark-green belly. A female. She looks around the square fearfully and runs toward the corpses. She tears the skin and pulls out fresh, bloody meat. A clattering can be heard from behind the wall. Splinters, stones, fragments of bricks and plaster, pour onto the square. The female withdraws hastily into the burrow.

I escape. I'm going back. The wind has ceased. I roam the deserted streets for a long time, careful not to be crushed by falling rain pipes and fragments of walls. In one of the streets, inside a still-smoldering car, I see a half-charred man, staring at me with glassy eyes. Gunfire begins nearby.

I reach the port right before dusk. My ship is still at the wharf. To my dismay, I see that the accommodation ladder is raised too high for me to get to it. I'm helpless. I run along the ship, looking for a way, for any entrance. Here it is. The ship's side is clearly outlined against the sky. Heavy mooring cables connect it to granite pilings driven into the shore.

The cables tighten, ease down, creak softly. The waves try in vain to move the ship, to push it away from the shore.

I climb the granite plinth and jump off it onto a cable that is thicker in diameter than my body. I wrap my tail around it, taking care not to lose my balance, and I ease up the cable. The black surface of the water glistens below. I hear the splashes made by fish breaking the surface to attack low-flying insects. If I fall, I'll drown or be devoured by predatory fish. The cable trembles, the vibrations become more and more violent. I dig my claws into the spiral strands and with my whole belly cling to the steep cable.

I'm halfway to my destination, but it is here that the vibrations are most dangerous, the tightening and loosening of the cable most noticeable. For a moment it seems that anytime now I'll lose my balance and fall.

I move slowly, the more so that the cable goes almost vertically up.

I can already hear people's voices from the deck.

As I approach, the black contour of the ship becomes larger and finally fills my field of vision.

I climb, helping myself with my teeth and tail. I embrace the cable with my paws, disregarding the sharp steel needles that cut my belly. Now I am close. A night bird flies by. For a while it circles. I freeze. I am an easy, defenseless prey. The bird flies away. I tense my muscles. My paws slide on the metal surface. Another moment, and with my nose I touch the cool surface of the ship's side. The fat cat resting on the deck purrs indifferently.

A fine, warm evening. Taking advantage of the lowered accommodation ladder, I go ashore.

The shooting is over, the city is quiet and dark, as if people had deserted it. That's an illusion. People are hiding; I sense their presence. A huge, glowing moon shines on the dead streets.

I head in a different direction than before, trying to remember as many details as possible. They will help me return to the ship. I encounter people more than once. They slink close to the walls, noiselessly, with no light. In this darkness I'm invisible to them.

Behind thick curtains, faint flames glimmer in the windows.

I turn into a narrow street — a strip between the gray walls. In this place, inside the gate, more light shows through the curtain. I squeeze my way in. A man is crouching on the carpeted floor. Above him, a large bird, a skinny hen, in a cage made of wooden staves. Clay jugs stand next to the cage. The man mumbles monotonously, mutters, rocks to and fro. I walk farther, taking advantage of the protection that his shadow affords me.

I get behind the wardrobe, I'm on top of it. From here I notice that the hen is sitting on eggs. That's why — most likely — the man locked her in the cage. If I could only get to her.

I try to jump onto a lower shelf.

The awakened hen has sensed my presence. She cackles shrilly, sticking her head through the staves. The man stands up, raises the lamp. The hen cries, thrusts her beak out as far as possible in my direction, strikes the jug standing close by. The clay jug shakes, tips over, falls.

I sneak out. In the street I hear the hollow sound of the jug crashing onto the floor.

You return to the port, you visit deserted houses, destroyed warehouses, stacks of barrels. You climb high piles of sacks filled with cement that has turned to stone, you roam the dark shore.

A dog has trailed you, he's following you. You hide under a boat lying nearby. You eat a dry fish left behind from a recent catch. The dog runs around the boat, sticks his nose underneath it, tries to squeeze in. To no avail. He sits, raises his head, and bays at the moon, which floats over the boat.

I am surrounded. The dog knows I'll try to sneak out. He

is watching. At last, tired, he puts his head between his paws and pretends to be asleep.

I run in circles over my confined territory, urinating in different places. The pungent smell of my urine will confirm the dog's conviction that I am still under the boat. Meanwhile I sneak out on the other side.

I run fast toward the ship, to make it there before the dog begins to chase me again. I can hear barking — he is circling the boat, convinced that I'm still sitting under it.

In a moment I'll see the huge shape of the ship rising above the shore.

That's right, this is the place. I run to the stone post marked with my droppings. Where are the mooring cables, where are the thick knots? I raise my head, stretch my neck, look for the dark contour. I run on the wharf to the place where I got off. The accommodation ladder should be here. It's gone. Only small waves crash against the shore. A little farther, a stone post marked by me. The mooring knot has disappeared from here as well. I go back. I run around the whole area. I search. The ship is gone. The sky slowly begins to grow lighter. I can hear the noise of the city that is waking up, the sounds of birds and people. I can't hide there. I can't stay here on the open wharf either.

You quickly find another ship moored nearby, and using the lowered accommodation ladder, you get inside.

I couldn't stay longer at any place, I escaped from everywhere.

Your whole life was an escape. You escaped from rats who hated you for your different smell, for the strangeness that infused you, for showing up on their territory. You escaped, thinking you were approaching the place where you began your journey, that city where your family had settled, where no rat would attack you or sense a stranger in you.

You moved from place to place. In baggage, loads, sacks, crates, containers, potatoes, grains, hay, fruit, rolls of fabric, bales of paper, on small and large ships, by train, in anything that provided a safe hiding place and moved, rolled, or sailed.

I escaped from rats, I escaped from myself, I escaped from people. I escaped seeking the flute's enchanting music. Ahead, in panic, in terror, with frayed nerves, ahead, farther, farther ahead. But the hostility of rats toward a stranger wasn't the same everywhere, and not all rats treated you in a similar way. For the most part, males attacked you, females less frequently, and it was never at the time when they needed a male.

In some cities the rats pursued me in a group, covering large areas in the chase. In their ferocity and hatred they disregarded other dangers that threatened them — people, birds, snakes, vehicles.

You were an alien rat — the most hated antagonist.

In other places the rats drove you away from their nests in the sewers and cellars, and from the areas where they found food. They let you stay there only at a safe distance from them.

Frequently, the rats didn't attack me at once; they allowed me to come close. That happened most often while they were eating — in a garbage dump, in a granary or a warehouse. The rats behaved as if my presence had escaped them.

I am eating peacefully, not suspecting the sudden change in mood that is soon to take place. A young male rat approaches me. He comes very close, touching my whiskers with his. He inhales the scent of my fur. He circles me, and when I think he is about to leave, he bristles up, jumps, moves his tail violently, issuing a high-pitched squeak. He tries to bite my tail. The mood of the other rats changes: agitated and furious, they run toward me.

The fiery, burning ball of the sun. I hate brightness, blinding glare, blazing and penetrating rays.

The light forces its way through half-open eyelids, through the skin, inside the skull. I feel it explode, spread, enervate.

I fear light. I was created to live in darkness, in shadow, in twilight and night.

I look around, try to find myself in the world of light, stripped of dusk and shadows, dazzling, blossoming, noisy, and clamorous.

This isn't a place for me. I couldn't live here, settle here, hunt. I couldn't.... The light would pursue me everywhere, it would expose me, it would kill me: each glare, each beam, each brightness and brilliance, as if a separate oppressor, a participant in a huge hunt bent on finding me, tracking me down, engulfing me.

Light means danger, terror, death.

My whole body trembles. Exposed, uncovered, defenseless, all alone with my fear, on the border of hysteria. I'm blinded, stupefied, broken. Surrounded by the blinding barrier of brightness, the wall that I can't cross, jump over, bite through, because it encircles me like a burning dome, like a lowered hot globe.

I have never seen so much light, such light. I haven't even suspected that there is such light.

The contours of my environment reach my brain through

the narrowed pupils. The heated, softened asphalt and scattered, rotting remnants of fruit, fish heads, shreds of scorched linen, gray pages of newspapers, dust, dirt, hot wind.

I sweat, my fur drips water — in a moment I'll melt in this heat.

The fleas bite mercilessly. They stick to my skin, squeeze into my pores, as if they were trying to hide inside, under my skin. They run off my back and onto my belly. The fleas that I brought on my body from the cold city.

At the end of the horizon a high concrete wall covered with barbed wire. Odd, strange trees, tall, with no branches, crowned with a mass of feathery leaves — they bend over this gray surface. I have to get there to survive.

I proceed toward the wall, along large tin crates that don't provide the least protection against the sun at its zenith. For a while I experience a violent urge to look at the center of the radiant ball. I turn my head and momentarily feel dazzled by the bright sky.

An enormous bird is wheeling high above, one of those dangerous predators that hunt anything moving.

In the field of my vision the border of the sunny disk appears: blazing, torturing, ravaging. At once I move my eyes away and stare at the oil stains evaporating on the concrete platform.

The sun has invaded my pupils, has left its pulsating afterimage, spinning circles that blur the scenery.

I fear the sun, I fear brightness, I fear space, I fear wind, I fear birds.

Life above the ground means fear, danger. A real life can only be lived deep inside, under the ground, in cellars and corridors, sewers and warehouses, in the system of waste pipes, in the interiors where the atmosphere is constant, immutable, undisturbed.

To reach the quiet underground labyrinths, submerged in darkness, in grayness, in mustiness. To get there fast, as fast as possible. To return, to find my city. The spinning circles slowly wane, disappear. The wall is already close by. I climb the scraped tin of the container, leap over the cement cornice, watching out for the barbed-wire coils. I slide down onto the other side, between walls made of cardboard and corrugated tin.

Rats, rats everywhere. The whole city belongs to rats, more to rats than to people. The rats don't hide, they come above the ground, run in full sun, in brightness, in sun rays.

I live in constant peril, in fear, under siege.

I avoid burrows, underground passages, sewers, labyrinths. I avoid them, yet all the time I encounter rats that immediately begin to pursue me.

I try to live on the border of the worlds — the rats' world and the human world — more above the ground than under it. I live in fear, vigilant and tense. But here the human world and the rats' world intermingle, mix, join, identify with each other. The rats are everywhere: inside apartments, in elevators, attics, gardens, streets, squares.

My tail, ears, and sides are covered with scabs of coagulated blood. If I hadn't escaped onto the sunny, burning surface of the asphalt, I would have been devoured, slashed, torn into pieces.

I have hidden in the reed roof of a clay house standing near the canal.

So far the rats haven't sniffed me, but how long will they

leave me here — scared, nervous, sick — between the bamboo beams, among the rustling, elongated leaves?

I hunted lizards and cockroaches, caterpillars and long, threadlike worms. I devoured decomposing fish heads and dog's entrails, dead rats and rotting fruit. I stole into garbage dumps and sewage pits, I escaped, slipped away, jumped, ran across the street. To be farther from rats, farther from rats.

I must return, I absolutely must return. Here I will be surrounded and torn to pieces.

I approach a ship. I want to reach the mooring cables or the accommodation ladder. The ladder is raised. Birds with long, dark beaks are circling above. I'll wait until dark. I hide among wooden crates.

Diarrhea. I'm losing tufts of hair. I have to return to the ship, to leave this hot, blazing city.

In the middle of a deserted street: dead people, bloodied, crushed.

Human flesh has a delicate, sweet taste that resembles the taste of pigs' meat. The sudden arrival of a truck interrupts your meal. You hide in the gutter. People throw the corpses onto the truck bed full of dead bodies. You can smell the heap of departing human flesh.

The night is particularly dangerous. Out of their burrows, tunnels, labyrinths, rats come onto the surface. The night — cooler than the day, gray and dark, seemingly peaceful — leads them into the street.

You remember: your attempt to get to the center of the city almost ended in tragedy. Walking the street with no lights, I approached a broad thoroughfare. At that moment I noticed many rats, which, disturbed by the presence of a stranger, were trailing me.

I dashed to the side, into a small street leading to the port.

My only chance was to hide among people, closest to the din and the light, to crouch in a place where the rats would be scared to attack me, to get into any inhabited house, to conceal myself in a corner and wait.

I ran in the darkness, followed by furious rats. The moment a large male grabbed my tail with his teeth, a car suddenly drove out of a cross street. The tire crushed the rat into pulp. The assailants stopped, and I got away.

I was near the port again. From a distance I heard the muffled splashing of the waves.

I had to find a suitable hiding place quickly. I smelled the approaching assailants.

I succeeded. People were asleep on mats woven from plant fibers.

A little human rested close by in a wooden cradle.

The snoring of the sleeping people and the gleam of the flames glowing in the dusk promised safety.

The rats that were pursuing me wouldn't break in.

I hid in the corner, in a small box next to the sewing machine. Weariness, exhaustion. I closed my eyes. I was resting. I recalled the cool, distant port, the brick walls, the hot oven pipes, the snow, the feather beds, the comforters, the pillows. Suddenly, the screeching of car tires. People were approaching. They were coming here. The door, pushed violently, fell in the middle of the room. It was gray outside. Soon a bright, sunny day would explode. The people got up, screamed, stood at the wall with their hands raised. Those who came in were ransacking the room. I slipped into a big clay pitcher just in time: the sewing machine was thoroughly checked.

Awakened, the little human started to scream. They took him out of the cradle, laid him down on the ground, close to the wall.

They tied the people's hands, kicked them, beat them, led them out. Lying in the corner, the little human kept screaming. I stayed in the pitcher. I waited.

Rats appeared in the room. I had to escape. I jumped on the floor.

The gray shadows moved toward the bundle with the little human. Intent on filling their stomachs with living human flesh, with warm blood, they didn't see me.

Through a chink in the stove I squeezed inside a long tin pipe that went to the roof.

I could hear the dying voice of the little human.

The snake freezes, motionless. He stares at me, raises his head. The black, forked tongue shoots out of his mouth again and again. He's readying himself to spring. I notice his muscles tensing under his dull skin.

In my city I once saw a rat being devoured by a snake. But that snake, which lived in a glass compartment, was much smaller than this one.

In a moment he'll hurl himself in your direction. He'll stretch himself like a long rope and then entangle you with his body, crush you, strangle you. When your vertebrae are shattered, your ribs broken, when you're dying, he'll take you into his wide-open mouth, he'll devour you, swallow you whole. A man had let the rats into a jar. They tried unsuccessfully to find a way out. The snake devoured them one by one; he watched their fear. Their attacks were futile, their teeth slipping on the hard scales.

A bird flying above distracts the snake. I jump aside in the direction that seems the safest: among feathery leaves sprinkled with dust. The snake jumps, lands right behind me. The thorny branches stop him. I have left gray tufts of fur and drops of blood there.

A high, dark mass towers ahead of me. After I get to the top I begin to feel violent movements. I am on the back of an ox, and that's where the cow's smell comes from.

The crushing blows of the tail, tipped with a tuft of hair, land next to me.

I move on his back, toward the head. The enraged animal gets up and runs forward. Clinging to his gray, rough skin, I have a hard time keeping my balance.

The ox stops. Squeaking, I fall over his head, hit the hard ground, rebound to avoid being trampled by him, turn around.

The face of a man with shining eyes and dark teeth. Sweat trickles down his skin. I can smell his feverish breath, I can hear groaning coming from inside. Stunned by the fall, I'm lying next to his hands. He'll kill me, throw me against the wall, crush me under his feet. He shoves me aside, leaves me alone.

Unable to move, I look at him. He falls down on the mats woven from plants. Blood trickles thinly from his mouth. He doesn't breathe.

I recover my strength, I escape.

Was I really there, or was everything a dream, a dream on the bottom of a ship, a dream during a serious sickness? In which port did that take place, in which city, in which stage of my life? It's hard to tell reality from dream.

Escaping from the rats that were chasing you, you forgot about other dangers as if they had stopped threatening you, had stopped existing close to you, were beyond the streak of light, the bend in the wall, the bank of the canal.

A moment ago you avoided death in the teeth of the local rats. You escaped almost at the last moment, with your hind paws throwing off the male rat that was already bending over your throat. Smeared with oil, with pieces of straw and feathers stuck to your back, you hid in a deep, dark hole in the dead slope of the hill.

The rats stopped, they didn't run farther.

I crouched in the circle of gray light seeping from above.

Then I saw a silent black shadow sliding quickly down the wall.

A spider the size of a large rat was moving toward me, followed by another one. I also noticed moving spots on the opposite wall.

Now I saw that the bottom of the tunnel was covered with dried, hollowed-out carcasses of rats, mice, bats, birds, lizards.

I jumped out. I escaped, avoiding at the last minute the hairy legs of the black spider.

At that time on the seashore, close to the port, I saw two large crabs claw apart the rat that had been chasing me. Before that happened, he followed me as far as the gray rocks protruding from the white fields of sand. From the stone block heated by the sun, I watched him bare his teeth and leap in my direction.

Suddenly two large, flat crabs appeared. They pressed him down to the ground, rent him apart, dragged him to their deeply hidden burrows.

You remember: one movement of the claws was enough, and the rat's head landed on the sand. The crabs fought with each other over the scattered bloody remains, dragging them around, separating them, cutting them.

I am again on a bright, sunny wharf near moored ships.

I have decided to sail away, to be far away from the hot, hostile city, full of unknown dangers, traps, masses of rabid rats, and sharp, blinding sun.

To get onto a ship as fast as possible. The sun begins to burn, and I feel drops of sweat trickling down the clotted tufts of my fur.

The ship is standing in the wharf, and the powerful arms of a crane are pulling platforms with wooden crates out of its hold.

Workers carry sacks down the accommodation ladder. I wander along the wall.

To find a place in a crate of copra or maybe in a sack of bananas. To gnaw through the board, to rip the sack.

I slink among the crates ready to be loaded. Maybe I could climb the accommodation ladder. But this isn't possible either. I find a half-eaten rat from the ship. He is lying with his throat cut, his entrails pulled out, blood coagulated on his teeth and ears.

Nearby I notice the outlet of a rat's burrow dug in the asphalt.

Suddenly a huge rat assaults me — a gray rat probably twice as large as I. I squeak, try to wrench myself away. He tries to grab me by the throat. I dig my teeth into his nose, I lock them. He breaks free, tearing the delicate tissue. I jump on the tire of a parked truck and then onto a platform covered with cement dust. I hide in the corner. I see a bird wheeling above.

Terrified, tired, hungry, I find shelter in an old coconut shell with holes in it. I stay in it till evening, ignoring the frightening heat.

It's dusk in the port. Only faint light illuminates the ship.

I wait for night to fall. Slowly I climb the mooring cable above the surface of the grease-covered canal.

At last the ship, the deck, the familiar places. Happy, I plunge into the whirring opening of the ventilator.

I hate the sea — its expanse, its calm, and its roughness.

The sea terrifies me like the sky, like the sun. It's a hostile element, dangerous, alien.

The waves strike the steel hull. Each of these waves may kill, destroy the ship, sink it. I am filled with fear.

The ship no longer seems a safe retreat.

The ocean is alien, contrary to my nature, adverse to my destiny, evil, insidious, superfluous.

I press my belly against a metal crate. I'm trying to fall asleep. The sea doesn't let me. It pours into me, splashes, crashes, tosses, rocks, groans. I can't forget the water from which I'm separated by only a few layers of steel.

A storm. The ship tilts, and the crates slide violently. To find yourself between them means death. The sparks of fear run along my spine.

What I fear most is being discovered, exposed. I fear the open space. I am then defenseless, disoriented. In such a situation every rat panics, runs ahead, loses orientation.

Cozy, narrow corridors, dim or eternally dark cellars, deep shelters, sewers with walls that are always damp — how I miss the spacious, safe labyrinth.

Although fastened down, the crates are moving. The clamor of loaded crates, the murmur of the waves, the distant hum of the engines, and the whir of the screw propeller.

In the cramped holds, close to the sea bottom, constantly rocking. The vibrations, the humming of the cooling devices, the shaking of the hull.

Despondent, weary, apathetic, I don't feel like eating or gnawing. My incisors have grown disturbingly long. I have noticed that other rats behave differently as well. Even the most aggressive and vicious have lost all desire to pursue, charge, assault.

Anxiety causes sleeplessness. I fall asleep for a short time, and immediately I'm haunted by cats, birds, snakes, numerous spiders, water streams, steel arms of cages, flames — they ambush me, pursue me, follow me.

I wake up at once. Both the sleep and the voyage exhaust me. I get tired, I fall asleep again.

In the depth of my sleep, a crowd of hungry rats is waiting. Their teeth get closer and closer. I run, but the rats surround me, spring on me, assault and bite me. I won't escape; I have no chance.

Again I'm on the street of a tropical city, full of spiders, poisonous insects, snakes. I'm running away. Suddenly the street breaks off. I'm falling. I squeak with terror. I wake up.

The ship rocks violently. The crates slide, creak, groan.

In that city the rats don't respond to my smell. Maybe it's that way because right after my arrival, I lived in a deserted nest and absorbed its smell, or maybe this is the city I've been seeking.

At the beginning I observe every precaution. I avoid venturing into cellars and sewers that are full of tunnels and burrows. I feed myself in the garbage cans, attentively watching the local rats, who act as if they don't notice me.

I'm still afraid that they will attack me unexpectedly. That's why I never enter their nests, why I never approach them or touch them with my whiskers. I have chosen the life of a loner.

I live near people, in their rooms. The thick walls of their old house conceal many cracks and crevices, chimney flues that are no longer used, and rusty air vents.

I have hidden under the floor on the highest level, close to the tin-covered roof. I often listen to the sounds coming from outside — it's the birds walking on the metal surface.

You've been here since the beginning of winter. A man who seems to be completely oblivious to your presence lives in the room.

Even the sharp grating of the teeth on a floorboard doesn't divert his attention from the spread-out papers.

A piano stands nearby. The man walks up to it and strikes the keys. Then he goes back to his papers. At first I had misgivings about the sharp sounds of that instrument. Now I have grown used to it, and I often run across the room behind the man's bent back. Every now and then he prepares a black, glistening, fragrant beverage. Its smell induces violent cramping in my stomach, because except for dried-out millipedes and papers, there's nothing to eat here. So you go down to the garbage can and drag up fatback skin, unfinished pieces of meat, chicken guts. You go no farther. That would be too risky now, in winter, when snow covers everything and hungry rats have a difficult time procuring food.

The man has noticed you. You stick your head out of a wastebasket standing near the door, in which as usual you haven't found anything. You jump on the floor, but he doesn't move in your direction.

In my sleep I smell the delicious aroma of cheese coming from the room.

I stick my whiskers and the tip of my nose outside. The cheese is lying halfway between the table and the burrow. I struggle with myself. I fear he wants to lure me out. He strikes the keys again.

111

Cautiously I leave the burrow, run toward the cheese, snatch it. I now notice a small bowl standing close by. I haven't drunk milk in a long time, in a very long time. I quickly carry the cheese to the burrow. The man is watching me, he has turned his head away from the keys. I eat the cheese and one more time go toward the milk. He's watching me drink. Suddenly he stops striking the keys. Scared, I escape.

Since that time I always find food on the floor. A piece of bread, cheese, or bacon, a fish tail. Milk or sometimes water in the bowl. I'm no longer scared. The man's attitude is friendly. He doesn't scream, he doesn't throw objects. I don't carry the food to the burrow anymore. I eat it on the spot. I know that the man is watching me.

Winter winds are blowing beyond the windows. Through the chimney flues and vents, they rush into the building, they howl and groan in the pipes. A moving, poisonous spider prowls around the room in search of sleeping insects and larvae. I see it walking on the bed of the sleeping man. It runs noiselessly across his face.

It's still winter. An awakening. As usual I go out of the burrow, in the direction of the food. Nothing is there. Only soured milk in the bowl.

The man is lying motionless on the bed. He breathes, pants, groans.

I hear steps on the stairs. The room is full of people. Scared, I hide and along the sewer pipes go down to the garbage cans, covered with snow.

The heavy boots make an unpleasant noise. All the time there are people in the room. I can hear them mumble, hiss, wheeze, and puff.

At night a candle lights the glistening face of the man who is lying down and the bent back of the person who is sitting nearby.

112

Again I find no food. I set off for the cellar. I satisfy my hunger with raw potatoes. Another awakening. The man is still lying down. He wheezes more, he coughs, he chokes.

Another trip to the cellar. The rats I encounter are no longer indifferent to me. They attack me. I go back. The room is empty. The man has moved out. The papers scattered in the corners have disappeared. The smell of the black room is gone.

The people are gone. Only the spider is spinning its webs in the corners.

Darkness, a plain of darkness. Darkness at the beginning, darkness at the end.

The wandering begins and ends in darkness. You return.

At the boundary, on the horizon, in the farthest perspective, a flame shoots out, a flash, a blaze spreads, devours the hills.

A strong wind, and the fires will burst with violent savagery — sudden, unexpected, scorching, and terrifying.

The currents of gas from decomposing matter explode underground, break out, ignite on contact with the air. People put the fires out, scatter garbage and sand on top, pour water, cement.

Fetid smoke oozes out from under the ground. Like fog, it hangs over the hills and even reaches the port. The birds then soar, become invisible. The clouds of smoke envelop me, sting my eyes and nostrils.

But here I am safe. Cloaked in the fumes from the burning dump, I get rid of my native scent, losing my sense of smell almost completely.

The rats that live here smell of fire, ashes, and smoke. They don't recognize their former, distinctive smell.

Permeated with the stench of fire, the fetor of burning, all the families live peacefully next to one another, without fighting, without kidnapping the young, without hate.

Yet when a strong wind blowing from the sea extinguishes the fires and clears the area of smoke, when humans pour truckloads of sand on the flames, when the fire disappears and the rain washes its traces and greasy soot off the soil — then we rats recover our former sensitivity to smells. Sensing no danger, we immediately begin to fight, fight for life against anyone from outside the family circle. We hate each other, we fight, we kill, we drive each other out.

That goes on until new bubbles of explosive gas from inside the garbage dump break through to the surface and the fetid smoke of another fire sweeps over us.

Liquid trickles down the tree trunk stripped of bark.

Above, a man is hanging — his head has fallen between his spread-out shoulders.

The scorching heat intensifies my thirst. Human blood, plasma, sweat. The dry wind deprives my gums of their remaining moisture. With my mouth open, stretching my neck, I steal up to the smooth trunk.

My nostrils smell the taste. I stand on my hind paws, lean on my tail, stretch my neck, move my whiskers, and stick my tongue out. I'm getting closer and closer. The dark liquid congeals in the heat, dries on the hot wood. In vain I jump around the trunk. The reflection of the sun blinds me. I fall on my front paws and cling to the sun-drenched ground. I rest. I try one more time.

Human blood would have quenched my thirst and nourished me. It would have given me strength.

You have ended up here by accident. The crate that was

pulled out from the ship was brought to this place. The intensely bright sand, the snakes creeping among the rocks. You must escape from here. You are a rat of dark corridors and shaded yards, a rat of dusk. You must escape as far as possible.

I try to get to the blood. I want to fill my bowels with the living liquid that will revive and increase my strength.

Yet the blood stops, sinks into the wood. I can't get to it. I circle the trunk, stretch my neck, jump.

A flying shadow will scare you away. You'll slide down the dusty slope of the hill into the hollow, among cars stinking of gasoline. There you'll find a scrap of paper, human feces, insects living in a sewage pit. You'll eat, get ready for the journey, for the escape.

When night's shadow bends over the earth, you'll try to go back there. You'll climb the hill, stand on your hind paws next to the trunk, you'll stretch your neck.

Instead of blood, you'll taste water, slightly salty, smelling of resin. Maybe it's rain, maybe it's stale sweat or urine. The man hanging above you is motionless, silent, dead. He poses no danger for you. A falling stone will warn you of a snake. You'll escape, rolling down and falling instead of descending.

Through an opening in the canvas covering the car, you'll get inside. You'll fall asleep. The whirring of the motor will wake you up.

You forget, you keep forgetting. The memories recede. Another chase, another escape. A ship. A city. Only now have I dredged up that place in my memory. I have recalled it together with other memories — uncertain, blurry, hazy, sickly — that keep flowing to me from darkness.

I squeak loudly, shrilly, trying to wake myself. My own cry and the warm stones under my paws bring back the

115

awareness of where I am, of the place to which I have returned.

But maybe I am there and the surrounding darkness is the warm dusk on the hill enveloped by motor fumes and smoke, the odor of gas and oil. I totter on the stony ground around the tree oozing blood. Burning thirst, aching, dry gums. And what's more, the wind — dry, hot, oppressive.

Danger everywhere. I don't know if in a moment I won't be attacked by a male or a female from the pair of infuriated rats. The female appeared when the ship arrived at a port of call. She mated with a young rat staying permanently on the ship.

They terrify the rats living here. They attack with rabid fury. There's no place to hide from them. They can appear at any place, surprise you at any moment. In the night I often leave the hold, and through the system of various pipes I reach the deck.

Rather than wait in the darkness of the hold for a sudden and painful attack that may end in my death, I prefer to stay in an open space. Because the rat couple has built their nest in my hold, I have become the main object of their attacks. They feel strong and want to take over the whole ship. They chase from place to place a few solitary rats that live here. They torment the other rats. Noiselessly they sneak up to a sleeping or eating rat and attack him from the side, biting his neck, springing on his back, biting his tail, the curve of his back, and his scrotum.

Their aggressiveness increases dramatically when the female starts getting ready to breed. Now it's difficult to find a safe nook because the couple wants to clear the whole area of intruders who don't belong to their new family.

Most of the time the male hunts the other males, the female hunts the other females, but often they attack together. Terrified, living under constant threat, exhausted by insomnia, the rats get sick, drop, die. In different places I encounter rats that are bitten, mauled, covered with scabs and wounds, ready to escape instantly, sensitive to every murmur and rustle. In the nooks of the engine room I discover the body of a rat with a deep wound in his neck. The rat bled to death. He escaped as far as the roaring, shaking sheets of metal. Except for the deck, this was the last place to hide.

I'm waiting for the ship to reach shore.

Every minute is filled with fear. It takes my sleep away, makes me weak and powerless. I find more and more rats that have been bitten and died of exhaustion.

We reach land. Except for the rat couple and their newborn offspring, I am the last living rat on the ship.

You have lost your way. In vain you try to break away from the ring of yards, cellars, boiler rooms, garbage cans, passages, pipes. Each attempt ends in my coming back. Upset over the futile attempts, I run, trying to recall the way I took to get here. I jump over doorsteps, slip through chinks, climb crumbling walls, and again return to the cellar that I have left. Stacks of crates, old furniture, rags, barrels, and junk create a very congenial atmosphere. But you can't stay here — the other rats will drive you out. I stop in front of an opening that leads into a nest. Maybe that's where another outlet is.

I leave. I fear sharp teeth, violent blows of the claws, shrill squeaking. I go out and come back to the same place again. I fall asleep on a stack of crates that reaches up to the ceiling.

Rhythmic sounds of music and stamping feet — heavy, loud, resounding. The tin plate of the lamp shakes right above my head.

When you hid under the surface of the sidewalk, the hum of footsteps above you . . . When you listened to the waves striking the iron hull . . . The shaking plate reveals a large opening that leads up. That's where the sounds are seeping from. They summon distant echoes, murmurs, hums. They remind me of the sounds of instruments, the whispers of water flowing in the sewers.

This is the way to leave. This is the way to get out. It grows quiet above. The sounds of footsteps subside. I squeeze my trunk into the chink. My body fills it up. I am under the floor of the room from which I can hear sounds coming. Maybe I'll be able to sneak out of here unnoticed.

A wide, well-lit chink between the boards. I jump out. People are here. I turn around as if looking for a chance to escape and, scared, scramble back into the chink.

You feverishly look for another way out. You go through the cellars you've been to many times, through garbage containers, sewers, corridors, vents. And again you are at the same place, at the same spot.

On your way, you escape from a rat that is eating a bread crust. You look at the walls carefully, examine the previously examined cracks and crevices. Here it is — an opening hidden in the dark.

Dull surfaces, hard yet gentle, lying close to each other, with no corners or edges. The corridors branch off, connect, cross, separate, come together. All of them lead to a destination. There are no blind walls you suddenly bump your head into. Each chosen route is the right one. It's enough to run ahead.

A gray surface before you reflects the light falling from above. The light doesn't dazzle the pupils with its sudden flashes.

Since the moment you came there, you no longer felt threatened, surrounded, ambushed, persecuted.

The little rats crawl over you. You shove them away gently, without anger. You crawl under a large, broad female. She doesn't push you away.

In the nest many rats are lying on top of one another.

This is your smell, your family, your great rat family, found at last.

How did I end up here? Suddenly. Unexpectedly. I must sniff, check, touch with my whiskers, convince myself.

The walls, the ground, the rounded edges, the holes gnawed in the boards, the hollowed-out corridors — they seem familiar, as if you had always lived here, as if you had never left.

Food, a lot of food — meat covered with blood, fat, cheese, fish, grain. The rats devour, gnaw, cut, separate, crush, chew, ingest.

There are no traps or poisons, no danger, no cats, people, dogs, snakes. All the animals are smaller than you, weaker, dependent. I kill a small bird, rummage through a mouse nest and devour the young mice.

I am a strong, agile rat, who is uncommonly fast and fit.

Between sleeping and waking, between waking and sleeping — at what place am I? Where?

The rats are devouring a dead human. They sit around him, they sit on him. They rip the flesh off the bones, eat the soft fat, the first layer of tissue under the skin, they pull out the veins, the muscles, the plexuses of nerves. They have reached inside. They cut the skin in several places, gnawing holes in it. They squeeze, crawl, slip inside. The corpse seems to have been brought back to life. We are in him, in his bowels. His skin is moving. We bore corridors in him, gnaw through the tissue and the membranes, the bones and the cartilage. Through his wide-open, already tongueless mouth I push toward the brain.

Suddenly everything breaks off. I am at the previous place — in the cellar to which I keep returning, under the noisy, vibrating ceiling. Cats scream, dogs bark, people mumble, musical instruments squeak and boom nearby.

I wait for the neighboring streets to empty so that I can wander farther.

In a tall glass container I notice a large white rat. He has shiny fur, slightly tousled on the back, almost transparent ears, and a tail covered with white down.

He is fat. He sits still; only his nostrils are moving.

He senses my presence.

I come near the glass. I rise up on my hind paws. He wakes up. He trains his eyes on me — eyes such as I have never seen in a rat. He opens his mouth, displaying long, overgrown teeth.

I gnaw at the pane. I hate him. I come here all the time after I wake up, the moment the people leave the apartment. I circle the transparent shape. I try to gnaw the metal welds. I run on the net that covers the top of the container. I try to raise it and push it off.

I can't get to the white rat, whose smell annoys me, disturbs me, infuriates me more and more.

120

The white rat is alarmed. He watches my attempts to get inside. Bristling, he walks back and forth along the walls of the container.

We look at each other from both sides of the pane. We press our noses and nostrils against it, we bare our teeth. I'd jump at his throat. I want to knock him over, to bite him, crush him, kill him.

My hatred doesn't subside. My anger will never find an outlet or be appeased. Separated by the glass pane, the rats scuffle, jump, issue shrill battle cries. The bristled-up hair, the wide-open eyes, the outstretched neck. He rests on his hind paws, leaning on his tail. With a whizzing sound he draws air in, picking out the hateful, hostile smells.

Never, never did I fight the white rat, never did I kill him, even though I desired and sought that. I was always separated from him by a steel net or a thick pane. Even though I tried many times to get to the other side, I never succeeded.

And yet I lived in their shade, almost among them, in the containers they occupied and filled with their smell.

White rats rise on their hind paws, stretch their necks toward me, leap, trying to reach the edge of the glass walls, gnaw the welds.

They are everywhere — in tall jars and transparent boxes covered at the top with a dense net, in cages made of steel rods. Their smell, intensified by the stuffy, closed rooms, arouses my hatred. My own odor is diffused in theirs. It doesn't exist, it doesn't even reach me.

They sit still, with only their heads moving rhythmically. They run along the walls or inside a rotating drum. Bristling, angry, full of hatred, I climb the nearest cage and walk over the net that covers it. I go over to another one, then the next, and still the next. Difficult to endure at first, the smell of a strange family stops bothering me. The rats separated from me by glass panes and nets live their own distinct lives. They can't do anything to me. They won't get out of their transparent nests, and I will never get to them.

Yet perturbed and ready to fight or flee, I hang around the cages, try to get inside, gnaw metal casings and rods. I press my nostrils against the pane, believing that it will come apart, open, disappear. But the nets fit snugly, the edges won't give in, the glass can't be moved.

After some time the white rats stop existing for me. I move between the transparent nests as if the rats weren't there at all. They grow accustomed to my wanderings, and now they no longer even raise their heads. Still and glum, they move their jaws rhythmically, devouring the food that the people bring them. They don't have to procure food. They don't have to kill, to hunt, to wander, to escape. The people hand them food, fill metal troughs with water or milk, carry the rats from one cage to another, stick long needles in their tails or necks. The rats shake and bend their necks.

The abundance of food lures and stimulates me.

I have settled under the floor. The house is old, full of unused chimney flues, vents, cracks and crevices. The heat spreads from below through the pipes.

It is cozy and peaceful here during the cool fall season, so I don't leave the building inhabited by the white rats.

The people prepare food in the adjacent room, laid with glistening, slippery tiles. Next to that room there is a storeroom, which I reach with no difficulty through a rust-corroded vent.

Dried fish, grain, peas, bread, vegetables. The white rats get everything.

122

They are sick. Huge black tumors distend the skin on their necks, heads, bellies. Small at first and barely visible, the tumors grow as if they were devouring the rats' bodies from inside, absorbing the muscle, tissue, bones. The tumors show under white, delicate hairs. They push out more and more.

The rats become thin, they shed, shrivel up. Some die quickly, others live longer, contorted, paralyzed, covered with dark growths.

The people dissect the rats, cut the tumors, look at the entrails.

He looks at me through the glass as if he didn't see me. A huge black tumor on his belly immobilizes him.

His tail and hind paws are in the air. He moves on his front paws, crawls to the trough, drinks. Right next to him is a female with a massive, ruptured tumor on her neck and a smaller one at the base of her tail.

Fear, fear that keeps increasing. The rats are dying. They roll over and in mortal convulsions kick pieces of carrots and bread. The couples copulate. Bodies covered with black tumors crawl on top of one another. The sick females have litters.

You watch it from another angle, from aside, from the perspective of your own life, which is not surrounded by glass barriers, not covered by nets, not fenced off, not enclosed.

You get used to the death of the white rats, to their slow dying. You are strong, healthy, fat. Your fur glistens. Your whiskers protrude, keen and sensitive. Your incisors cut the toughest wood and lead cable casings. You are afraid no longer. The death of the white rats doesn't imperil you, it's beyond you, beyond your fear.

The people come here rarely, only in the morning. I am

123

mostly asleep then after my nightly roamings. I wake up when they leave the building again.

You watch the people, you watch the white rats. You venture out into the attic. There are many boxes here, clearly marked with rats' droppings. You enter an opening, turn into a side corridor. A blind wall stops you. You withdraw. You enter from the other side. The same thing happens. You search for another passage. Straight ahead. Wrong again. You check the first route. You are right: there is a passage before you reach the end. You exit from the other side. You try again. You don't find the way at once. Only during your second attempt do you pass with no trouble.

The exits have different shapes in other boxes. Suddenly you are imprisoned. You rattle in the small space, trying to pry with your nose the tin hatch that has fallen down after you.

It's a trap. I am in a trap. I run, check the corners, fling myself at the walls, bang my head on the glass pane that covers the crate. I fidget.

Suddenly, after I press it, one wall rises. A short corridor, and I am on the other side.

During my next stay in the attic I walk inadvertently into the same box. The situation repeats itself. For a short time I can't get out. Storming about doesn't help, even though I touch each spot. Later the wall gives in. This second imprisonment has scared me. I remember the box and don't enter it anymore.

The people carry the boxes to the adjacent room and place them in such a way that the white rats have to cross them to get to the food and the drink. I watch them through the glass from above.

A gray local rat appears in the cellar. We sniff each other,

124

we touch. He issues a shrill cry and springs at my throat. In the corner of my eye I notice another rat. The fight is lost. I have to escape, to leave the warm, comfortable lair and wander away.

For a while I hide in the attic. By diverting the assailants' attention, the white rats save me. Starved, I go down. The gray rats are gone; the people have scared them away.

They return at night, gaunt, hungry, cold, and aggressive. Through a hole in the cardboard that covers the cellar window, I get outside. Freezing wind hurls snowflakes at me.

You will be expelled from here as well. To continue going across the cemetery is purposeless. Fed on decomposing human flesh, the rats that live here will not let me stay. It's safe and peaceful inside, under heavy slabs, deep underground. Food is the most important, so much food — meat, fat, cartilage.

A rat treading the stone edge jumps off, comes up to me. Our whiskers touch. A violent cry. An escape.

A new journey awaits you. You'll search for the city the existence of which you begin to doubt. You have no choice, you have no other choice. I have to leave.

Rats connected by the tips of their tails, grown together, stuck together. Each pulls onward. None turns back to cut the tip of his tail with his teeth. You watch them. They remain in a large box, like a motionless gray flower. Well fed, fat, they don't have to look for food. The people place food under their noses. That makes them completely lethargic.

In the corner I discover a jar of liquid with an offensive odor. A sudden fear. The traps I have seen in the cellar indicate that the people look for rats, that they need rats. They replace the old and ailing rats with the new ones.

Stupefied, the fat rats sleepily watch me dart across the glass pane that covers the boxes. I run down.

I relieve myself on a trap. I jump up on a wire cage and watch my droppings fall on an aromatic fish head. This is a warning. No rat will enter it now.

Through a half-open cellar window I get outside. In the garbage container, among orange peels, I notice a roll of paper wrapped with a cord. I gnaw, cut, shred, until scraps of paper remain, particles blown by the wind.

The roar of the sea reminds me that I have to leave the city and look for more congenial regions. I walk toward the sea.

Nearby, in a round building made of stone, I find a bowl with milk that has turned sour. I eagerly eat even the tiniest bits. The port, the ship, are not far away from here. From close by I can hear the characteristic hooting of the sirens. I leave the stone building and run along the shore toward the sound. I try to run as fast as possible, away from the stone rubble inhabited by rats. The wind carries their alien smell.

Cautiously I emerge from the barrel. I run across the broad empty floor. I slink outside through the broken glass pane. I rest in the sun, next to a large garbage dump. I experience an immediate gnawing hunger. I listen carefully to what is going on around me, to check if there is unforeseen danger. Muffled by the walls, the howling of a locked-up dog comes from the nearby buildings.

Apart from that, the surroundings seem safe.

You climb a brick wall and slip between the heaps of decomposing fruit, rotted cabbage heads, skins, guts, and scales. You throw yourself at the food. The overabundance of wonderful-smelling delicacies almost stuns me. Among them I forget the danger. I eat very calmly, feeling delightful warmth in my belly and in my bowels. The buzzing of large, shiny flies makes me lazy. They settle here and there in a compact dark mass.

Suddenly I feel a strong blow in my side and a sharp pain in my neck. A furious rat has bitten me abruptly. I assume a defensive position, but he attacks me again, with such a force that I roll over onto my back. If I hadn't thrust him away with a strong kick of my hind paws, he would certainly have killed me.

He issues a piercing cry — a signal that a stranger has appeared.

Another rat jumps on my back. He is much smaller, and I knock him off easily. At the same moment still another rat appears. I bolt in panic, knowing that the local rats, alarmed at my presence, will now try to track me down. Jumping out of the garbage, I encounter a large male.

I escape along the wall of a warehouse. Terrified, I avoid all burrows and openings. In this situation they may turn out to be the worst trap. Driven into a cellar, a sewer, or a nest, I wouldn't have any chance of survival. I don't know the area. I escape blindly, fearing, despairing, wanting to save my life. One moment I feel a strong bite on the lower part of my back. The pain gives me strength. I flee along the walls, across the open space. I suddenly end up among trees with low-hanging branches. I know that my enemies are following me and if I don't find a hiding place I will perish. Taking advantage of the thickenings and scars in the tree bark, I climb the branches and scare some birds off. I cower among the leaves, which are shaking in the wind. The completely unfamiliar environment and the possibility of

127

falling down or being discovered by a predatory bird terrify me. But those sensations dissolve quickly, because the rats that have been pursuing me show up under the tree. With bulging eyes and hair bristled up from excitement, they run among the trees, bumping into one another, biting, sniffing, continuing to search.

More and more tense, exhausted by fear, I watch them from above. They prowl near, annoyed at the sudden disappearance of the stranger.

At this moment, when I am on the brink of complete exhaustion, close to death from fear and anxiety, other rats come running and attack my enemies with hatred, biting them and chasing them away. I remain long among the branches, waiting for the rats to stop fighting and disperse. If I went down now, I would be attacked immediately and most likely torn to pieces.

You are in the strip between two zones occupied by rat families that constantly fight and kill one another.

In the evening, terrified when a dark bird with a powerful beak appears nearby, I climb down the tree. The rats are gone. I don't know which way to go. The space between the areas that belong to different rat families is small, and I can be attacked at any moment.

I rest motionless next to a dead rat. Fear overwhelms me, yet I have to reach a ship and escape, get away from this place. I hear a rustling sound.

I am so scared that I disregard the bird wheeling above and again hide among the branches, a place contrary to rats' instincts and foreign to our inclinations. Yet only here do I feel secure now.

*   *   *

The old rat has no strength. His back was once broken, and he is dragging his legs. I circle him, attacking him and jumping off. I plunge my teeth into his side, into the skin at the base of his tail that covers his testicles. He squeaks during each attack, carefully aiming his bites.

Now I bite him in the most sensitive spot, on the side of his neck. I feel my teeth tearing a vein that runs there. The old rat tries unsuccessfully to reach me with his teeth. He is growing weaker and weaker, more and more terrified.

He rolls over onto his side, trembles with fear. Blood flows from his wounds and his mouth. He dies. He was the only rat inhabiting a small ship that you got on after a long, forced stay among the branches. I killed him right after I arrived, when the ship's sides were still bumping against the shores.

A night bird scared me away from the tree. I could choose: either dying in the bird's claws or making my way to the port. I ran as fast as I could toward the fishy-smelling wind. The rats that I encountered started immediately to pursue me.

In the port, at the wharf bright with moonlight, there was only that ship, still, black, quiet. Its sides were below the level of the wharf. When I jumped on the deck, the wood made a hollow sound.

A decrepit rat living here showed up at once and attacked me with fury. He thought that I would run away, that I would get scared and leave. You couldn't run away. The rats from the warring families were lying in wait on the shore.

I am sailing. The loud roaring of the engines reaches everywhere. I take over the old rat's cozy nest, wedged between the layers of wood and metal. He has cushioned it with rags and scraps of paper.

I am sailing. Staying in such a small area all the time

irritates and upsets me. You didn't know what lack of movement and space meant when you were in large holds. Here it is different. People are present everywhere. Only at night, when the sea is calm and the people are asleep, may I freely sneak across dark interiors filled with cardboard boxes that exude an unpleasant smell of tobacco.

I know this port: the wharves, the low buildings, the dust carried by the wind — everything seems familiar, as if it were emerging from a dream. But it isn't a dream, even though several times already, on awakening, I have had a sensation that reality may be just another dream which I inhabit, in which I live, exist. It isn't a dream; it's just your memory.

The ship has come to the shore. I'll wait and disembark. I've had enough of running in a small space between the creaking sides of the ship.

It's night already. I quickly run down the lowered accommodation ladder.

The huge, glowing moon lights the strip of the wharf and the outlets of the nearest streets. I was here. Back then the city was burning, explosives were going off. Now it is peaceful. People are strolling on the streets. I can hear the distant meowing of a cat, the barking of a dog.

I hesitate. Should I go farther or climb onto the deck of another ship, avoiding an encounter with local rats, cats, dogs?

I decide to look for food in the closest sewers and garbage dumps. The delicious, sharp smell of a dried fish lures me.

A pile of dried tails, heads, guts. Greedily I eat the fish bones and dry gills.

The first rat has already approached. He is small, with a long trunk. He sniffs me. Squeaking, he alarms others. He bites me at the base of my tail. I turn back and plunge my teeth into his leg. He jumps off. He is bleeding.

130

The rats don't pursue me. They are satisfied with driving the intruder away.

The walls blackened and scarred by explosions. I remember this city. The moon shone in a similar way when I was slinking across the deserted, darkened streets.

Now there are many lights. Mumbling human voices and music can be heard.

All the time I have a sensation that I have once walked the same road, on the same rough pavement, among dust mixed with dry dung.

People walk close by. I press my body against the wall and remain so for a while. What am I afraid of? Grayness makes me invisible. Yet I am afraid. It's the encounter with the rats that has filled me with fear. I recall the tall branches of the tree in which I hid in the panic of escape.

I myself have often pursued strange rats, I have inflicted wounds, I have bitten, I have killed. I know this hatred very well, the hatred of an intruder, an alien, a stranger heralding the arrival of others, who from those that are pursued and attacked may easily turn into those that pursue and attack.

Squeaking reaches me from inside the sewer. Fear seizes me. I don't know the area well. If they begin to pursue me, I have little chance of escape.

I turn into a street that is paved with oval stones, shining in the moonlight. I know this street, I know it very well. But what happened here?

Dim light penetrates the gate where a ragged curtain dangles. This sight is also familiar. I slip inside. A man squatting on the carpet catches a jug that is falling from high above. He puts it away. Suddenly I remember everything. I was present when this jug fell. A hen is perched in a cage made of wooden staves and placed on a shelf. She cackles loudly, sensing my presence.

So everything that has happened since the moment I escaped from here has lasted no longer than an instant, no longer than the falling of a clay jug.

You did hear the hollow sound of the jug shattering on the floor. You heard it, but you don't believe, because the moment you came here the same man caught a falling jug right above the floor. Maybe I have fallen asleep, maybe everything has been a dream — the cities, the roads, the travels, the pursuits, the escapes. What dream could abound in so many events?

So I am again at the outset of my wanderings, after a long voyage in the holds of a ship carrying sugar, after leaving the city in which the flute player died.

The man notices the dashing rat. He grabs a lead weight. He throws it. I escape.

Vexed, I run around the house. In the corner of the garbage container I discover the shards of many broken jugs. It was a delusion — that jug broke into pieces back then. The man has now caught another jug.

Furious, angry squeaking can be heard around me. Rats are encircling me. They come closer and closer. I bounce off a hard shard and jump over the wall. I don't stop until I get to the strip of bright shore.

Barely alive from exhaustion, uncertain if the rats have really stopped pursuing me, I look for a shelter.

Along the rail of a port crane I run toward massive metal vehicles covered with matte tarpaulins. A few movements of my jaws are enough, and I get inside through the opening I have gnawed.

Every attempt at leaving the hold fails. The hatches fit snugly and don't allow the smallest crack through which I could squeeze. I try in vain to gnaw through dense nets and closely spaced bars that protect the pipes. I am in a trap, a huge trap full of steel machines placed close to one another.

Death by starvation is imminent. I eat everything that is fit to be eaten: scraps of paper that I find inside the metal constructions, oily linen rags, dry wood shavings, a few tiny insects, ants and spiders that got in here by accident, dried bird droppings stuck to tarpaulins. The hunger remains unsatisfied, it burns my insides.

Thirst tortures me most. I suck moisture from the lowest layer of wood shavings covering the hold. I drink the oily liquid that has collected at the bottom of the steel constructions. It's too little. Thirsty and hungry, after a long search I discover a trickle of liquid seeping down the wall. The water is salty, full of tiny rust particles. I wait for the drops to gather, to swell and flow down.

I live like that for a long time, a very long time. Terrified, at the beginning you run around, constantly looking for an outlet. Despair and fury choke you. You try to climb the walls of the hold, but even though several times you reach the steel plates that close it at the top, you don't find a single chink.

On my hind paws, leaning on my tail, I often stand on the metal construction and stretch my neck up. I try to smell the odors coming from the kitchen, to hear sounds proclaiming that my anguish will soon be over.

The trip continues. I bear the rocking of the ship well, but the storm terrifies me: especially the violent lashing of waves against the side of the ship and the enormous lurches when the thick steel cables strain and moan as if they are about to break. A long time after the storm is over I feel painful cramps in my neck and back.

I am the only rat in the immense hold. I constantly move

along the wall, checking every inch of the surface. I also examine the interiors of all the steel vehicles. Suddenly — it keeps happening more and more often — I can hear clearly the grating of a rat's teeth, the rustling sound made by an animal moving under the tarpaulin, a piercing battle cry, as on an island that I have left. Often when I am asleep I sense the touch of the whiskers and the warmth of the nostrils of the rat that is sniffing me. At first I wake up immediately and begin a long, feverish search.

I haven't found even the slightest traces of a strange rat's presence in the hold, even though I have checked all the corners and nooks. Yet the illusions recur, interrupt my sleep, my rest. My reactions to the sounds of the nonexistent rat become more and more violent. Whenever I hear a rustle or feel the touch of the whiskers, I hurl myself at him with hatred and fury. I chase him, pursue him, trail him.

I am sick. Dejected, again and again shaken by feverish chills, I sit on a pile of shavings. I feel gnawing and burning in my bowels. Anything I eat comes out of me in the form of thick mucus. I grow thin, I lose hair. Bleeding blisters that quickly change into hard scabs have appeared on my skin. Painful itching of my skin forces me to scratch. Moving my leg or raising my claws toward my back tires me, irritates me, weakens me.

If it weren't for the bothersome itching, I would gladly remain still.

Thick mucus with a salty taste flows out of my nostrils and into my mouth. I breathe with increasing difficulty. I sneeze, spit, cough.

I become more and more apathetic and sleepy. I huddle, indifferent to the rocking of the ship, the assaults of the storm, the distant blowing of the wind, to the voices of my own imagination, to delusions and dreams, to memories, to the acute itching of my skin, to hunger, thirst, pain.

You have stopped grooming and picking fleas. I am dying slowly, and even though I know it, I can't defend myself. I can't defend myself, I feel I have no chance, locked up as I am in a tight iron box.

Fleas begin to run away from my molting, feverish fur. They sense my approaching death. What is there left for me? — I eat a worm wiggling in the sawdust. I freeze, still. I roll onto my side. I wait. . . . I wait. . . . I fall asleep.

I wake up suddenly. The rocking has stopped, the engines no longer roar. The muffled sounds of the port cranes come from outside.

The steel hatches covering the hold open. The light that I haven't seen in a long time blinds me. With a final effort I slip into the dark interior of a vehicle.

People descend into the hold, touch the cables, talk.

Surrounded by thick armor, I am lifted high. A cold wind rushes inside. After a while the rocking stops. I am on land.

I hear clattering, roaring motors, the cries of flying birds, an unfamiliar humming and rustling.

I want to live, I want to live. . . . On tottering legs I sneak out from between the steel sheets. I run toward the port warehouses.

Sick, feverish, half dead, sore, I am squeezed into a corner. I have no energy to pick out with my teeth the fleas rampaging on my belly. Their bites are painful. They stick little needles into my skin, drink my blood.

More and more enfeebled, resigned, terrified, I am lying in my shelter, deeply hidden in the labyrinth of passages and burrows.

I can hear a rustling sound. . . . It's the rat from the adjoining burrow, who has come to see what is happening — if I'm alive or dead. He withdraws. He has smelled my sweaty, feverish skin.

A rustling sound again. What if it's a snake. There are no snakes — no snakes here. Snakes will never come here. The stench of the sewers, the decomposing remains, the fetid water, will hold them back. And yet I am afraid of a snake even here, in a place that seems safe and tranquil. The rustling grows distant, passes, fades away. I'm trying to sleep. I rest my head on my front paws, I straighten my hind paws, I stretch.

My fever increases. I fall into a huge pit. Like a bird, farther, lower. Sudden fear. Death waits down below, in the well. I'll hit the unfamiliar bottom, the water that has the hardness of concrete when one falls from such a height.

I squeak, cry, try to hook my claws onto the smooth walls, glistening with moisture. I curl up into a ball and abruptly straighten up.

Unfortunately, the walls are glasslike, with no protrusions. With dazing speed, I'm falling. Am I dying? I am in my old family nest. I'm playing with the young rats. We are squeaking.

The entrance to the nest expands. The wide-open mouth of a snake. In a moment he'll devour me.

I squeak, I try to run. To no avail. The huge opening covered with hundreds of flat scales bends over me, pulls me in, devours me.

I wake up bathed in sweat. My hair is stuck together and bristled. The fleas are still biting. They walk on my whiskers. I drive them away with my paw.

Everything has been a dream, a hallucination, a delusion. Ailing, wasted, I'm lying in a cool place between the storage area of a large store and the rainwater drain. I'm having chills. I feel burning thirst. To drink, I have to get out of here and reach the stone wall, dripping with water. But will I have enough strength? Shaking and staggering, I reach the corridor. I am slow, I am cautious.

With difficulty I reach the cracked stone wall. Water is trickling, drop by drop.

I press my lower jaw to the wall. I raise my head.

I haven't drunk such cold water in a long time. I'm taking my time, trying to soak up all the water. From my throat the water penetrates farther down, fills up my stomach, cools my hot blood. I feel better, much better. Immediately I try to get at the fleas.

I have recovered. New hair has covered the bald spots. The abscesses have healed and scarred over. My strength is coming back.

During the first part of your stay in a new city, the sickness probably saved your life. The rats left you alone, sensing the fever and the sharp stench of diarrhea. After being locked in the dark and stuffy hold, the surrounding world seems bright and loud.

A slice of bread and sausage skins pulled out from greasy paper taste as good as if you were eating them for the first time in your life.

Such abundance of food has caused a complete upheaval in my organism. I'm awakened by sharp, violent pains in my distended and hardened stomach, by diarrhea and vomiting.

Again I fall into a deep, feverish sleep. After I wake up, I feel fine. And what's most important — I have recovered my former uncontrollable appetite.

I hide in a tall building close to the canal. A vibrating sound of bells comes often from its towers. This sweet tune reminds me of the faraway sound of the flute.

But the main reason that I have decided to stay in this tall building, where hawks have nests in the towers, is my fear of rats. Since you recovered, they have been tormenting you again.

Incessant hunting for rats that arrive from the sea is taking place in the port.

The whole neighborhood is inhabited by a family of large and strong rats, which fiercely track any intruder that appears in their territory.

If it hadn't been for my fever and my frightening smell, they would have killed me right after my arrival. That's why the present place, far from warehouses, elevators, granaries, and garbage dumps, is without doubt the safest. Searching for abundant food, the rats rarely come here. They know that except for some garbage, mice, stalks of various flowers, and candles, they won't find anything to eat.

Every day I satisfy my hunger with what I find in a garbage container that stands near buildings surrounded by several rows of fruit trees.

I live in a hollow plaster figure. I enter through an invisible opening in the base. Groups of noisy people that occasionally gather here make me uneasy at first. But since their presence is related to the sounds of music that is pleasing to my ears, I adjust quickly. I remain inside until the people leave.

In no time I also get used to the safe, quiet interiors.

The hollow plaster statues, the thick candles, the flowers in glass vases, the dimmed lights, the quiet, the stone floor.

I would stay here longer, but one day the statues are taken

138

down, the floor is covered with canvas, scaffolding is erected next to the walls.

Again I feel a sudden urge to search for my own rat family, for the city where I was born, for the old bakery and the cellar with the walls bearing the traces of cemented burrows. People stay inside the tall building all the time now, and I constantly feel threatened.

I wander away at night, running along the walls of the houses, the garden fences, across the squares and streets. I am running away from the distant sound of roaring waves carried by the wind, from the smell of the sea and the noise of the ships sailing on the canal. I am running toward my city, toward my first nest.

The cities are alike. I arrive and leave mostly at night, always pursued by rats.

The rats from my family will recognize me at once. I'm waiting for the moment when the rat that I approach won't spring at my throat, won't issue a ferocious cry summoning the members of his tribe to pursue me.

I wander, I move from place to place. The urge to return to the places I left, the need to find them, my memories of them, compel me to wander.

Maybe it is the last city, the last of those that resemble so much the city of my memory. But I am unable to determine at once if those are the same cellars, the same sewers, the same underground passages, the same gutters. I don't recognize them. I have come here at the beginning of winter, and the first icy winds have driven me deep into the sewers.

For a long time, in all the cities, you have searched for the bakery on a back street, with the cellar into which coal was poured from above. In that cellar, on the wall, near the faucet, there are traces of cemented rat burrows.

You have less and less time. You're getting old, you're losing your sense of smell, your hearing, your sight. A moment ago you attacked a spider, thinking that it was a millipede or a beetle. You are no longer strong, you have grown weak. You run more slowly, you jump lower, you tire sooner.

I avoid danger. I get out of rats', cats', dogs' way. I don't attack piglets and hens. I eat bread crusts and pieces of fat that get deposited on the banks of the canals. I avoid store-rooms and pantries in apartments. I fear being caught; I'm afraid of death.

My dark fur has turned gray — along the back, near the ears, on the sides. My claws are brittle. The incisors grow more slowly, and what's even worse — they break easily. A while ago an upper incisor broke suddenly on a hard oak board that you were trying to gnaw.

My whiskers, which until now have guided me unerringly in complete darkness, suddenly begin to fail, to bend, to break. Not long ago they protruded stiffly around my mouth. Now they have dropped, they are drooping.

I have grown old. I feel that in every muscle, in every bone and tissue.

Old age is simply a great weakening, limpness, and exhaustion. It's a disease of time. I defended myself against old age. For a long time I acted as if I were still young.

My testicles no longer swell with sperm at the sight of every female in heat. It's been a while since I had my own permanent nest. Besides, I don't feel aroused, I don't feel this overwhelmingly strong urge to copulate, the urge that once incited me to fight, to wander, and to search. After my last sea journey my sexual urge weakened, and recently it has disappeared.

In the sewers of the city where I am now, I have discovered a burrow that branches off into a comfortable, broad nest. The heated surface of a thick pipe filled with warm water forms one side of the nest. The burrow is inhabited by a single young female, who walks around me exposing her blood-filled sexual organs for so long that I finally copulate.

I have interrupted my journey. The burrow is cozy and warm. The female that I have met has almost made me younger, has reminded me what kind of male I used to be. The streets, the cellars, the sewers, seem familiar, as if seen before and remembered. I have stayed.

Biting cold, thick snow, winds that penetrate everywhere, are not propitious to wandering. As a result I don't leave the area close to the sewers.

A new generation of young rats is growing. Several of the most curious ones haven't come back from their first trip. You huddle on the warm concrete slab, warming your belly and paws.

You are more and more afraid. You fear the maturing male who attacked you a short time ago and bit your ear. You wanted to stop him from copulating with your female, his mother. A strong sense of ownership stirred in you, although you are no longer a young rat. The young male jumped on me, knocked me down, mauled me. My ear is painfully swollen. You cower with your head bent to the side and watch the young rat wooing your female.

You wanted to have your own nest, to be the leader of the rats living in it, to drive intruders out of your territory.

It happened as it did because it couldn't have happened

any other way. You are an intruder in your own nest, a weak old rat approaching the end of his days, of his possibilities. Your female has already stopped being your female; she is now the female of the young rat. She has kept you off a hen's head that you have fished out of the sewer, and together with the young male she is eating the delicious brain. You won't even stir to drive the rival out.

They will drive you out, throw you out, expel you, shove you out of the warm burrow onto the cold edge of the sewer. The young rat hates you, continually circles you, wants to attack you. Only indifference saves you. Otherwise he would have attacked you long ago, trying to knock you over and bite through your artery.

I leave the nest reluctantly, but I can't stay here. I have no chance in a confrontation with the young rat.

The morning sun, spring but still cold, dazzles me.

It's early, the day is just beginning.

The street and the wall along which I'm walking seem familiar, as if I had been here in the past, as if I had seen it all before. Even the stone edge of the gutter and the grate of the drain covers.

Where did you see that? I don't remember.

Through a wide crack between the pavement and the metal gate, you get to the yard with the cast-iron pump in the middle. The smell of flour, fat, and hot bread is coming from the buildings that surround the yard.

A bakery is located here. From that roof it's easy to get to the storeroom, full of provisions. That door leads to the room with a huge oven. Here, a little higher, there should be a window to the cellar. Now it is covered with a pile of iron pipes. The window is tightly boarded up. There is no entrance here.

You are almost certain now — this is the place, the bakery,

the house, the cellar. All winter I lived so close to the place I wanted so long to return to. If you had come above the ground sooner, if you had earlier visited the neighborhood . . .

The garbage containers are different from the ones I remember. The place where they stand has been surrounded by a brick wall. I sniff the brand-new items. From the roof of the annex I try to get inside through the storeroom ventilator, but the opening is covered with an iron screen nailed to the wall. I decide to climb the rain pipe to the roof and get to the cellars from there. I move up in the narrow pipe, taking advantage of all irregularities of the tin. I have succeeded. I am already in the attic.

I make my way to the staircase. Everything here is different: bright, luminous, smelling of paint. I quickly slide down the steps. I listen to the noises that are coming here. There are no cracks or holes in a restored, renovated building. What if people saw you on the stairs — a large rat, balding from old age, with a long, hairless tail and nostrils that display his sharp teeth. The door to the cellar is ajar. The pungent odor of paint assaults my nostrils.

In the corridor you catch sight of the familiar hard floor. The sewage pipes have been covered with a layer of plaster and paint. The space between the pipes and the wall is gone.

In the cellar you will stop at the wall next to the faucet. The wall bears no marks. Covered with oil paint, its surface glistens in the dusk. Was the burrow here or there, or maybe in the place you have just passed, running from one corner to another, or maybe a little farther? Is it this cellar for sure? Where is the coal? The faucet bubbles in the same way, sun rays shine through the hatch placed high overhead, dim light seeps in through the small window covered with a metal screen.

Have you really found your city, the place where your old nest, your first burrow, was? I run around the cellar many times. The drain is covered with a new tin hatch. It's impossible to squeeze in there. The crumbled bricks have been replaced, the sides have been reinforced with an iron plate. Maybe in the neighboring cellar you will find the old, familiar objects.

In the adjoining cellar the same wooden shelves stand next to the walls. There are different jars, filled with appetizing food. The wooden carcass of an armchair stands in the middle. Sniff it carefully, examine it. You will find the marks of rat's teeth left by the female who built her nest here. Here are the marks. So you have found the place of your birth. From here, from these cellars, I set off on my journey, from here I wandered off.

The rats that I met in the sewers, the rats that drove me out of the nest, are my family. I have found what I have sought. I have found it.

Go back to the other cellar, stop at the wall, right behind the faucet. Listen to the sounds, the echoes, the rustling, the scratching. Listen. You have come here believing the impossible, believing that you will hear the grinding of the teeth, the grating noise of the mother futilely gnawing the wall with her teeth. I huddle, cling to the wall with my side, close my eyes, listen.

You won't hear anything. You can't hear anything. You know it perfectly well. The burrow in the foundation of the bakery was sealed for good, and no noise can reach you from there.

The mute, silent, dead wall. The reflections of light slide on the floor. I feel hungry and thirsty. The smell of bread being removed from the oven aggravates my hunger.

You turn toward the well-known passages, chinks,

corridors. They are gone, there are no traces of them. They have been sealed, painted, smoothed over. Metal screens that fit the frames snugly have been installed in the windows. Only the doors to the cellars have remained unchanged, and with some difficulty one can squeeze under them.

I can get out of here the same way I got in, the most dangerous way.

The smell of fresh bread increases my intense hunger. I feel a gnawing in my throat and in my stomach. I'm climbing the stairs. You hear steps moving from the upstairs toward you. The sound of running water comes from a small corridor next to the landing. I jump there. Maybe I'll get out of here through sewage pipes, straight to the sewers. I hear screaming in a brightly lit room. The man sitting in the tub is yelling. He lets others know that I have broken in. He throws a brush and a bar of soap at me, he splashes the water. Another man, standing in the doorway, tries to catch me when I'm darting close to his legs. I dash into the apartment; I hear his steps behind me.

You have hidden behind the couch. The man moves the furniture. He finds you. The stick strikes right next to you. I jump onto the balcony, the same balcony where at one time a cat watching the yard was sunning himself. The man follows you. You try to slide down the wall, you can't, you leap. The contact with the stone surface is painful. You twist your hind paw, roll over, get up. The man from the balcony is yelling at the people below. They are running. You are escaping straight ahead, trying to find any opening where you could hide. Right in front of me I see many round openings. Those are metal pipes, lying in the yard. Limping, I dive into one of them and run toward its bright end.

It's unusually noisy inside the pipe — the sounds and

echoes from the yard, the street, and the neighboring buildings meet here, merge, surge, bounce, clash. The rustling of my fur and the grating of my claws on the hard surface are suddenly magnified.

The bright end is approaching; it's almost here, within reach of my whiskers. Suddenly a piece of metal blocks it. I hit it with my nose, my head, I bite it, I scratch it. I have fallen into a trap. I hear people's voices. I turn back with difficulty and run quickly in the opposite direction. The pipe rises, tilts. I'm sliding, falling down. I see a man's eyes in the light toward which I was running. I hear his mumbling, coarse voice. Now both ends are covered. The people shake the pipe, tilt it violently, strike it, causing unpleasant noise. They turn it.

Terrified, with my paws apart, I'm trying to keep my balance. But it is impossible — there are sudden tilts, turns, and twists. I vomit from fear. They stand the pipe upright.

I turn, dig my teeth into a narrow chink, trying to widen it.

They raise the pipe again. Again they toss it, turn it, shake it.

The light, at last the light. I'm running to the bright end. I fall into a small wire cage in which I can't change my position. You have been immobilized in a metal trap.

The thin steel wires cut your gums. You bite the board. You struggle, squirm, squeak.

The people are watching you. They are mumbling. A sharp stick is stabbing your side. In vain you try to grab it with your teeth. They throw in a piece of bread, but hunger has stopped bothering you. They carry you near the oven. The terrible heat increases your unquenchable thirst.

The people are watching. They shake the metal cage.

From the table he picks up a long, thin butcher knife that

is sharpened on both sides. He raises it. He carefully examines its blade.

They want to maim me, they want to kill me. I dig my paws into the board, I push my back into the metal bars until I feel pain. Trapped, immobilized, I can't do anything. They are approaching.

The blade flashes over my head.

Finally they push the knife through the bars of the cage toward my head.

They want to reach my eyes. I move my neck rapidly. They insert the knife from the bottom so that the blade, pressing on my throat, immobilizes my head. They pull a red-hot thin wire out of the oven. It's coming. The eye senses the growing heat, the glow, the brightness, the fear. They thrust the wire into my pupil. The pain explodes in my skull.

I squeak with all my strength, with the last of my strength.

Now the hot wire touches my other eye. It enters inside. Everything turns into darkness, turns into pain, blood, sound.

I wake up from a prolonged torpor. I get up. I am in the yard. I feel the hardness of concrete with my paws.

Darkness, like the darkness after birth. Similar yet different. Back then it was the darkness of ignorance, of unawareness. I knew nothing except darkness. Now it is the darkness of a life's crisis, the shadow of approaching death.

Back then I didn't know about the existence of light, about its force and brightness, about dusk, about humans, about myself. I had no presentiment of the events that were soon to take place.

Later, terrified by light, I sought dusk, shade, the musty and stuffy atmosphere of cellars and sewers.

I didn't know that I was a rat surrounded by awesome dangers, by traps, enemies, by my own ruthless community.

I feel painful stinging in my eye sockets. The blood no longer flows into my mouth. For a moment I stand still. I'm blind, condemned to finding my way by the touch of the whiskers.

They didn't kill me. They poked my eyes out and left me alive in the yard. The stinging becomes more acute. I fall down, roll, grab stones with my teeth. Everything breaks off.

I have noticed it from far away.

It's lying on a smooth, even surface, not the slightest elevation around it.

It is round, huge, the largest egg you have ever seen, but you also feel stronger, more deft, capable of any effort.

You sniff the glossy shape carefully, you walk around it, you brush against it, you try to scratch the smooth surface. The egg pulsates, smells of a bird, of the life inside, of the yolk, of the white, of grub.

I must roll it to a safe place, crack it, eat it. You wrap your long, powerful tail around the egg and begin to drag it behind you. Suddenly the surrounding area inclines, and you realize that you are rolling the egg uphill on an increasingly steep slope. For the time being the egg rolls obediently behind you. It doesn't resist or slip away. You feel a sudden pressure in your tail.

You turn around, and to your dismay you see an oval stone. When did it happen? When did the transformation take place? Where is the egg? Careful not to let go of the stone, you turn and support it with your side. You scrutinize its structure and its surface. It's a stone that has been polished by a current of water. Resigned, you close your eyes.

In front of you there's again the egg, magnificent, glossy, aromatic, ideal. The stone has undergone another transformation.

Now he is pushing the egg upward. With his head, his side, his paws and teeth, digging his paws in and propping it up, sliding, slipping, straining his muscles and arching his back. It's harder and harder, more and more difficult. He's growing weaker. In a moment he will yield to the increasing burden.

You see your own tired back, your fur molted from age. A strange, unknown, different rat is pushing a shiny egg before him, fascinated by its size and smell. An egg that is transformed into a stone, a stone transformed into an egg. It's you, nobody else but you.

How can I see anything if I have been blinded, deprived of my eyes? How can I see? Yet I do see. I am arduously pushing the shiny ball before me.

The ridge of the hill appears on the horizon. In a moment you will approach it. You will roll the egg onto a broad surface full of hiding places and burrows. There, by rolling it on a sharp pebble, you will break it and eat it.

Right before the ridge, you discover that there is no egg, that it doesn't exist, that there is no stone either. The enormous, increasing burden is only your imagination, pure delusion, fancy. That's what you think. You believe that, you are convinced that neither the egg nor the stone exists. At this moment, right before the summit, before the place of rest and respite, the rat — you aren't sure if he is you — stops pushing on the weightless shape, invented and hence nonexisting. He turns and looks down.

Do I or don't I see? Am I blind or not? Or maybe it's not the eyes that see the world. Maybe.

The enormous egg is falling down the slope. It's rolling noisily on the surface, which is as smooth as a mirror. You see it from above, dashing, returning to the place where you started on your way.

Everything around you begins to drop. The slope, the hill, are no longer here.

Everything is on the same level — both the egg and I.

From a distance you see it roll more and more slowly. It stops, it grows still. It is close to or almost at the same place where you first saw it. Go near it, start over. You know what it smells like inside. It lures you, woos you, tempts you. Start over; it's such an easy prey. I have no more strength, no more strength. I can't see anything except darkness. I can't even crawl.

My head is hurting, the empty sockets under my eyelids are hurting, my neck is stiffening. I feel chills on my back. I'm lying in the full sun in the hot yard.

The people have left me. I rise, I stagger, I walk. I bump my head on a brick, I stop, I slowly move along the wall. I hear voices; people are talking. They are watching my behavior.

I'm seized with panic: they may kill me, crush me, trample me. They may do anything to me. Unsteadily, on shaking legs, I circle the yard. I have lost my sense of smell. The blood flowing out of my eye sockets has stopped up my nostrils. I don't know where to go, but I have to get to my nest and to the sewers.

I find a furrow with water flowing in it. Human voices accompany me all the time. I reach the drain. My paws feel the metal ribs of the grating. In this place, between the cast-iron bell-shaped drain and the broken stone curb, water has eroded a convenient descent. I can hear the people approaching. Would they want to catch me? I hastily crawl into the crevice. The way down is now too steep for me to descend. I fall.

I roll down, inert, half conscious, lifeless. I bump my head on a protruding corner of a brick. I stop on the sloping roof of the sewer.

A stream, surging after a rainstorm, flows in the sewer below me. I hear small waves striking the concrete edges.

Blood streams out of my eye sockets again. I taste its warmth in my mouth.

It's cold. There's confusion and pain in my head, constant painful spinning.

A rat comes near, walks around me, touches me with his whiskers. He could kill me, cut the fragile thread of life, life that still goes on. Water is flowing from above. There must have been another rainstorm. The noise in the sewer increases, intensifies. Unfamiliar murmurs, whispers, echoes arise.

The water cools off the feverish skin, washes off the congealed blood. I feel better, but I continue to lie motionless, stupefied, feeble, sick.

You didn't foresee, you didn't predict such an end. But how could you have known that something like that would befall you, that they would blind an old rat soon to die somewhere in the corner? He's lying here like a piece of old rag or a dead pigeon. But you are alive — you still exist — suspended between the foaming stream of sewage and the crumbling roof of the sewer, between living and dying.

The flowing water slowly restores my strength, my will to live. How will you live without eyes? You will recover your sense of smell, you'll smell many familiar odors in your nostrils, you'll breathe them in. The smell will direct you where necessary, it'll tell you where you are, it'll explain what surrounds you. You do have your whiskers, long, gray, stiff, extending at each side. You remember how faultlessly you moved in the dark, guided only by their touch, by their resilience when they encountered an obstacle.

I want to reach the nest. He drove you out. You were thrown out by a young, strong male, like the one you were not too long ago. It's difficult to accept, difficult to part with the vision of the warm walls next to the pipeline of the heating plant. . . . You'd like to die there, nowhere but there.

Don't accept that expulsion, but don't go back. He'll bite you, choke you, kill you.

The female doesn't need you. She now has an exceptionally lustful, large rat, which she herself bore. He'll leap at your throat.

But you want to return no matter what. Now, lying still in the rivulets of water running down the walls, you want only that.

You return on shaky, unsteady legs. You crawl into the burrow, reach the nest, lie down next to the warm wall and rest.

You will wait for death, you will wait for the end.

I move my paws. I shift on the clay ground, trying to assume a normal position. The headache doesn't relent. The stiffened neck weighs much more than usual.

Thunder resounds nearby, a short distance away, high up. I can feel the earth tremble. You'll open your eyes and see the grayish, dim light.

I open my eyes, close, open again, close, open again. Nothing . . . I don't have eyes. Can I grasp that?

But where does the ray of light come from that — as if from under my eyelids — forces its way into my brain?

Where does the afterglow, the reflection, the shadow, come from? You don't have eyes. You are a blind rat dying among damp, crumbled bricks.

He turns. He almost falls down into the rippling stream of sewage. He turns, leans against the slippery, clay-covered wall.

The thunder is gone. It has rolled and faded away. Its light doesn't matter, it makes no difference, its power has declined. Now I don't fear the thunder. I don't fear it because I will never see the lightning again. Blindness has eradicated your fear, has removed your fear of what in the past forced you to flee.

You roll over onto your paws. You feel the muddy surface, you support your weary body on your tail. You cling to the ground. Raising your heavy, wounded head is too taxing for you.

You have recovered your smell. The odor of rainwater and of the vapors rising from the sewers fills my nostrils.

Quench your thirst with the water running down the walls. The fever isn't over yet; your jaws are shaking. Drink, drink for a long time, drink.

With my whiskers I will examine this place to make sure that nothing threatens me here, that I am safe, that the bricks won't collapse under my weight, that the wave flowing from high above won't wash me away.

The rainstorm is over. You have to go down, eat a grain, a piece of fish, the crust that you have found. You have to fortify yourself.

You won't recover your sight; that is impossible. People have gouged your eyes, have bored through your pupils with hot wires. You won't revoke it, you won't escape it.

I raise my head, stretch my neck, carefully sniff the space around me.

Your strength will come back; just wait. The rat that you have encountered many times will pass you. You'll pick up your strength and bite him when he begins to sniff you. He'll run away squeaking. He'll avoid you, he'll be afraid.

He's running away. You hear his claws scratching on the bricks. You try to clean your fur and catch a few fleas. The muscles in your head are still hurting. They sting when you touch them. Why are you cleaning the eyes that aren't there? The pain knocks you down. You are lying on your side and shaking from bitter cold.

It is night above the ground. The air has cooled off. Day and night now mean the same darkness, which you will never penetrate.

You have slid lower, steering clear of the hole in the roof of the sewer, through which you could have fallen into the dense stream of sewage. You squeeze through the narrow opening and stand at the wall next to the brink.

You are returning to the nest from which you have been expelled, the nest where the last generation of your rats has matured. You are returning to the place that is no longer yours, yet you are returning to it.

I'm approaching it, it's nearby. With my whiskers I find the entrance and go into a long corridor that runs upward. For a moment I lose my sense of direction in the system of underground tunnels. Finally I reach the nest. The female and the little ones sniff me. I hide in the farthest section, in the blind tunnel that protects me from all sides. When the young male attacks me, it'll be difficult for him to drive me out.

You are tired, extremely weary, as if after a long sleepless journey.

He lies down, making himself as comfortable as he can, among scraps of paper and dry leaves. His eyelids have sealed up the empty sockets, and he no longer feels the pain, the stiffening, the stinging. He is resting, falling asleep, submerging in his own dreams, wanderings, memories.

He sees himself there, his whole life, spinning, confused, but at the same time appearing more clearly than everything he has seen before.

So I am dying. Is that what it is? Don't be afraid. You are only falling asleep and experiencing your life one more time, but this time inside, within yourself. You find the lost threads, the insignificant episodes, you connect the distant fragments from different places, paths, and moments. Inside, within you, time and space converge, shrink — what was before and after doesn't matter.

From the back of a gaunt ox I jump right in front of an old, dying man. He stares at me with his black eyes, deep like tunnels in which I could hide.

Music: that's right, you can hear music. Listen to it attentively: it's the flute from the city on the sea. The flute has been found; you hear its tune more and more distinctly. It intoxicates you. In a moment you'll follow it wherever it leads you.

The jug falling down, knocked off by the wing of a bolting bird. You run away, and in that time you cover a long distance, see bright landscapes, a city on fire. And when you return to the same place, the man catches the falling jug right above the floor.

It's a delusion. There are plenty of disintegrating shards of broken jugs.

Suddenly you see people lifting an old tattered armchair.

The dog is barking furiously. Little rats fall out of the armchair; they perish under the heels of the shoes.

On a bare hill with no vegetation, people are nailing a man to two crossing tree trunks. They leave him under the bright sky, hanging on the post driven into the rocky ground. Come near, lick the drop of trickling blood.

Don't fear the bird that is wheeling above. He doesn't see you; he is staring at the dying man.

He let me out. Why did he open the metal hatch of the cage? What happened then? Or maybe it's only a dream. He is standing, watching me escape, run away. He doesn't move, he's only watching.

You find the outline of the fresh cement patches on the wall. A muffled scratching comes from inside. It's the mother, trying to break through, to gnaw through the wall. You know well that she won't have enough strength, that she'll die from lack of air and water, immured in the nest in which she gave birth to you, in which she gave birth to your rats.

You begin to bite, to gnaw the hardened, rough wall until your jaws ache and bleed and your teeth wear down to your gums.

Why are you gnawing, since you know that it is hopeless, futile, senseless? Your lifetime won't be enough for you to gnaw through that wall. You will come here many times, listening to the sounds from behind the wall, listening to the sounds that now live only within you.

You are leaving this place forever. A snake from a faraway city is pursuing you. He encircles a rat with his coils, crushes him, shatters his bones, and now devours him, opening his jaws wide.

A throng of rats plunges into the river. The river is gray, vast, boundless, covered with small waves. The rats want to swim to the other side. They arrive, push the rows of rats that are ahead into the water. They won't be stopped.

I am among them, I swim, I swim, I swim. . . . Around me the rats grow faint, drown, pulling their companions down with them.

Swim, don't give up, you have enough strength, swim. Any minute you'll see the riverbank on the horizon.

An unknown force strikes you — maybe it's a wave or maybe the young rat wants to drive you out of the nest.

He keeps swimming; he's closer and closer to the bank. Keep on. You are swimming ahead; this is your longest journey.

Have I recovered my eyesight? Maybe I never lost it.

What is happening to you? Where am I? Many rats have crossed the river. They are still wandering, crossing lands, crossing seas, wandering.

As at the beginning, I'm pursuing the light. It is distinct, bright, dazzling. I'm running toward it. You are following it as you followed the music of that flute. I'm crossing cellars, sewers, labyrinths, farther and farther, on and on.

For the first time I feel safe, secure, peaceful. But maybe you are the light — gray, animate, predacious.

Could the young rat have bitten through my throat, could it be my blood that's filling up my throat? I don't feel pain, I'm running ahead in the brightest tunnel I have ever seen. What a magnificent moment, what a magnificent moment, what . . .